Truth Or Dare
RUMOR
CENTRAL

Also by ReShonda Tate Billingsley

Rumor Central

You Don't Know Me Like That

Real As It Gets

Published by Kensington Publishing Corp.

Truth Or Dare
RUMOR CENTRAL

RESHONDA TATE BILLINGSLEY

Dafina KTeen Books
KENSINGTON PUBLISHING CORP.
www.kensingtonbooks.com

DAFINA KTEEN BOOKS are published by

Kensington Publishing Corp.
119 West 40th Street
New York, NY 10018

All Kensington titles, imprints, and distributed lines are available at special quantity discounts for bulk purchases for sales promotion, premiums, fund-raising, and educational or institutional use.

Special book excerpts or customized printings can also be created to fit specific needs. For details, write or phone the office of the Kensington Special Sales Manager: Kensington Publishing Corp., 119 West 40th Street, New York, NY 10018. Attn. Special Sales Department. Phone: 1-800-221-2647.

KTeen logo Reg. U.S. Pat. & TM Off.
Sunburst logo Reg. U.S. Pat. & TM Off.

ISBN-13: 978-0-7582-8957-5
ISBN-10: 0-7582-8957-X
First Trade Paperback Printing: June 2014

eISBN-13: 978-0-7582-8958-2
eISBN-10: 0-7582-8958-8
First Electronic Edition: June 2014

10 9 8 7 6 5 4 3 2 1

Printed in the United States of America

Author's Note

W ell, here I am again, wrapping up Book 4 in the *Rumor Central* series. I can't begin to thank you guys for showing me (and Maya Morgan) so much love. I love creating the good, the bad, and the downright scandalous drama that Maya seems to keep getting herself caught up in.

It's such a blessing to be able to do what you love. And I've been a lover of the written word since I was a little girl. So to be able to do this on a daily basis is a dream come true.

Some people don't know this about me, but I wrote my very first story two weeks after my fifteenth birthday. There was this magazine called *True Confessions*. It was actually an adult magazine (don't tell my mom), with all these scandalous stories that women found themselves caught up in. They had a call for stories, so I submitted a story about how I stole my sister's husband (the stories were supposed to be true, but of course, since my sister was only twelve, I'd made mine up). I never expected to see that story published. I just wanted to make up something. So, imagine my surprise when I got a letter from the magazine saying that they loved my story and wanted to publish it! They sent me a check for a hundred and fifty dollars. (I never cashed that check because I didn't have a bank account and I was too scared of my mama.)

Unfortunately, I set my dream of writing on the shelf, and tried to pursue something "a little safer." If I have any regrets in my life, that would be it—to have a love like I did for writing, but not explore it because I wanted to "be safe." Oh, I could've been safe, and still pursued my passion on the side, and not hung it up altogether. So, for all you aspiring young writers, keep writing, keep believing, and keep putting pen to paper.

As usual, I can't wrap up without a heartfelt thanks to some very special people in my life. To my children, Mya, Morgan, and Myles (notice how I use their names in the books ☺). Thanks to the rest of my family; my friends; my agent, Sara Camilli; my phenomenal editor, Selena James; my bomb publicist, Adeola Saul; and all the fab folks at Kensington.

Much love to my friends and sisters of the teen pen who also craft wonderful reads for young people, Stephanie Perry Moore, Ni-Ni Simone, Nikki Carter, Shelia Goss, and Victoria Christopher Murray. Make sure you check out their teen books as well!

Thanks to the terrific readers who pick up my books, tell others, and show me so much love. Big shout-out to parents and grandparents like Bettie Beard, Marsha Cecil, Jetola Anderson Blair, Joan Estinval, Danyelle Brown-Schulze, La Tonya Mavins, Beverly Harper, Sharla Lewis, and all the adults who always make sure they are putting my books in their children's and grandchildren's hands. Major love to all the other parents, teachers, librarians, reading and literacy specialists, and concerned adults who turn teens on to my books. Keep spreading the word and I'll keep writing!

I can't wrap without sending a huge shout-out to my social media followers. You guys keep me motivated, inspired, and encouraged! I wish I could name each of you personally, but how about you just insert your name here: _____. A thousand thanks to you!

Make sure you shoot me an email at reshondat@aol.com or follow me on Instagram at ReShonda Tate Billingsley and let me know what you think about *Rumor Central*. Can't wait to hear from you. Now, get to reading. The next book in the *Rumor Central* series is coming soon!

Much Love,
ReShonda

Chapter 1

I couldn't stop smiling as I watched the commercial with white sandy beaches, crisp blue water, and hot-bodied people walking up and down the beach. In just a few days, that would be me (of course I would be a lot cuter than that busted-looking chick in this commercial). But I couldn't wait. *It was about to be on!*

"Stand by," my director, Manny, said, snapping me out of my daze.

I turned back to the camera to get my shine on (not that it ever left), but I got into serious focus mode when the camera turned on. As the popular host of the hottest celebrity gossip show—not just in Miami, but in the country—I always had to bring my A game.

"And we're back in five, four, three, two . . ." Manny pointed to me as the *Rumor Central* theme music came up.

"What's up, everybody?" I began. "It's your girl, Maya Morgan, and we hope you've enjoyed today's edition of *Rumor Central*. You'd better believe that we're all over this latest story about Usher, and you'll want to make sure you keep it locked here to get the latest scoop. But you'll have to tune in in two weeks because your girl is out! That's right, I'm heading to Cancun, Mexico, for a little fun in the sun, rest and relaxation, and an all-around great time at the world-famous Spring Break Fling! Check out this short video from the Fling last year, shot by none other than one of the members of the boy band Four Dudes."

On the video, stars were partying with regular people in what looked like the best party ever.

The weeklong Spring Break Fling had been going on for a few years, but in the past couple of years, young celebs started going and that took things to a whole other level. Granted, I was going with my senior class, but I wasn't about to tell my viewers that. I didn't need the world to see I was getting excited about a high school thing. But make no mistake, I was pumped. The only thing that could've made this better was if my cousin, Travis, were going. Despite some drama with his drug-dealing friend last month (long story), I loved kicking it with my cousin, who had come to live with us earlier this year. Travis was fun with a capital F, but he was going back home to Brooklyn, New York, for spring break to spend time with his sick mother.

No worries, though, because the party must go on!

Manny gave me the cue to wrap, so I said, "Yours truly will be all up in the mix this year, so you know it's gonna be fiyah! Enjoy the break. I know I will. Until next time, holla at your girl."

The theme music came up again as the credits started rolling. I couldn't get my earpiece out of my ear fast enough.

"Bye, Manny," I called out, not bothering to wait for a reply. I was so ready for a vacation. Since I'd started as host of *Rumor Central,* I had become a workaholic, which wouldn't be so bad if I weren't seventeen and in the prime of my teen years. But hey, you couldn't be on top—and stay on top—like me by being a slacker. As Diddy said, "I'll sleep when I die." So, I wasn't making plans to sleep in Cancun, but I *was* going to kick it. Even though my girl Kennedi didn't go to school

with us in Miami (she lived in Orlando), I'd managed to fina-
gle her on to this trip. (Hey, when you were a rich chick like
me, you made your own rules.)

Anyway, between Kennedi and my other BFF, Sheridan—
and of course the fact that I *was* the life of the party, any
party—we were about to have a blast.

"Looks like somebody is ready to go," my executive producer, Tamara, said, approaching me as I speed-walked down
the hall back to my office. As usual, she was fly in a burgundy
custom-tailored Vera Wang pantsuit. Her jet-black bob had her
looking ready to kick butt and take names. I guess that's why
she was the top dog at *Rumor Central*—next to me, that is.

"Well, that's the understatement of the year. I am so ready
to get out of here," I replied, stopping to face her.

Dexter, the show producer, stood next to her smiling mis-
chievously. Dexter was Tamara's partner in crime and ever
since they'd canceled *Miami Divas*, a reality show that I had
starred in with four other people, and given me my own
show, they were always conspiring with one another.

"Uh-oh," I said, my gaze darting back and forth between
the two of them. Whenever Dexter got that look in his eyes,
something was up. It meant his mind was churning.

I glanced at my watch. I had fifteen minutes before I was
off. So I didn't need his mind to be churning with anything
concerning me.

I decided I wasn't even going to ask questions. "Umm,
okay then, I'll see you guys in two weeks," I said, trying to
step around them.

"Hold on," Tamara said, following me. "We're going to
walk with you to your office."

I looked back and forth between the two of them. "I'm
off in fifteen minutes." They gave me a lot of respect, and
sometimes, I could tell the older people at the station had a
problem with me being only seventeen years old, but I'd
more than proven my worth. In the beginning, people used

to doubt if the gossip I delivered was legit, but they had quickly learned that I was right on the money with most of the stuff I brought to the table. Being in Miami's "It Clique" had allowed me that luxury.

"This will only take ten minutes," Dexter said, giddily, like he was hiding some big secret.

"Okay, what's up?" I said. I walked in my office and started gathering my things. I would listen, but I didn't want to stop and make them think I was giving them too much of my time.

"Well," Tamara said as she exchanged glances with Dexter. "We know you're about to head to Cancun with your friends and so Dexter and I were talking . . ."

Dexter was so excited that he couldn't even let her finish. "And we think now would be the perfect time to take the show on the road."

"Excuse me?" I said, finally stopping and giving them my undivided attention.

"Think about it," he said. "Maya Morgan in Cancun at the Spring Break Fling with young celebrities from all over the country? Oh, that's some good juicy material waiting to happen," Dexter said.

I couldn't believe they were going there—again. When I'd first started the show it was bad enough that I'd had to turn my back on my *Miami Divas* costars. Since she was my best friend, Sheridan had since gotten over it. But the others—Shay Turner, Bali Fernandez, and Evian Javid—were still salty about it. So, I'd felt bad about that (for a brief minute anyway), but then I'd had to sell out my friends for ratings and that had created major drama. Now, here they were asking me to do it again.

Dexter must've been able to tell my mind was churning because he said, "You talked about wanting to go international. This is the perfect opportunity."

Tamara continued. "I was talking to someone and they

told me a whole lot of young celebs go to the Spring Break Fling. It's become a hot spot for them to let their hair down. That sounds like some good stories waiting to happen."

"This is supposed to be my vacation!" I protested.

"Sweetie, do you think Beyoncé takes a vacation?" Dexter said.

"Ummm, as a matter of fact she does," I replied.

"No, trust and believe, I assure you, she's still working even while she's on vacation," Dexter said.

"We're not trying to take away from your fun. We're just saying now would be a perfect time to have a camera crew go on the road," Tamara interjected.

I shook my head. I was so not feeling this idea. "I just want to relax and have a good time."

"And you can," Tamara said. "If we send a camera crew, we're footing the bill."

I looked at them sarcastically like *that* was supposed to be enticing to me. I could foot my own bill. As a matter of fact, this trip had already been paid for.

"Everything's already taken care of," I said.

"So, you have the penthouse suite of the InterContinental Presidente?" Tamara asked matter-of-factly.

"How do you know where we're staying?"

"Honey, we know everything," Dexter said, folding his arms and flashing a sly smile.

"Well, no, I don't have the penthouse suite. We tried to get it, but they told us it was unavailable."

Both Tamara and Dexter smiled. "It's unavailable for normal people. Not for a network like WSVV," Tamara said.

"So picture yourself in the penthouse," Dexter added. "I mean you're already the 'it' chick and I'm sure you have a very nice room, but we've booked the whole top floor of the InterContinental Presidente. The penthouse suite just for Maya Morgan."

That made me raise an eyebrow.

"We'll make sure you have a driver, unlimited food and drink—non-alcoholic of course—everything at your disposal. We know you can do all of this yourself, but why bother? Let us do it for you," Tamara said.

I narrowed my eyes. "And all I have to do is agree to let you film the trip?"

"That's it," Dexter said with a smile. "Let us film it and *Rumor Central* gets the scoop."

"And we'll even give you your free time," Tamara added. "Just get us enough for a few stories and the rest of the time is yours."

I wasn't feeling this idea because I really had been looking forward to just relaxing, but images of the penthouse suite, a driver at my disposal, and an all-around good time on someone else's dime made me say, "Fine I'm in."

I hoped it wasn't a decision that I would end up regretting.

Chapter 2

"Ain't no party like a spring break party 'cause a spring break party don't stop!"

I laughed as several of my friends sang our signature It Clique song while the baggage handlers loaded our luggage onto the party bus. I'd invited along a select group—the "in" crowd—and they were all hyped when they saw the bus.

My friends and I had really been hyped the whole plane ride here to Cancun. Most of us travelled quite often—all over the world, in fact—but it was nothing like being able to spend a week on a sandy beach with your friends. Yeah, we had some chaperones, but we had made it very clear that with the kind of money our parents shelled out for our exclusive private school, Miami High, those chaperones were just here to make sure nobody died and nothing more.

"Come on, Maya!" Sheridan called out, heading toward the bus.

Kennedi had already gotten comfortable in the front seat. I wanted to laugh. That was so Kennedi, staking her claim. I was just about to say something when I saw the cameraman and sound guy from my station approach us. I'd known they were sending these two and one undercover cameraman. I hadn't warned any of my friends that *Rumor Central* was sending a production crew. I knew they wouldn't be happy about it so I wasn't going to say anything until the last possible moment. And it looked like the last possible moment was here.

"What's up, Maya?" the cameraman, a guy named Quincy, said as they walked up to the van. "I see you guys just made it."

"Yeah," was all I could say.

"Our flight just got in, too," Quincy said.

Sheridan and several of my other classmates stopped in their tracks, looked at them, at me, and then back at them.

"Oh, unh-uh," my friend Zenobia said. "Is that a *Rumor Central* crew?"

"I know they're not here to film us," Shay said.

I wanted to tell Shay that she was lucky to even be on this party bus, since I didn't like her ghetto-fabulous behind anyway. She was only here because I'd invited her and Evian Javid. Our relationship had never been the same since all of that drama with *Miami Divas*. Sheridan had gotten over it. Bali had moved away. And while I was back speaking to Shay and Evian, we weren't cool like *that*. Still, I invited them along because I was trying to be the bigger person (and of course, I wanted them to see how I was rolling).

"I know that's right, no filming," Sheridan echoed as she handed her Vera Bradley bag to the driver. She turned to face me. "Please tell me they are not here for work."

"Chill," I said to everybody standing around staring at me. "Yes, they are here for work. We are taking *Rumor Central* on the road, but this is actually a win-win for everybody."

All of them gave me a "yeah, right" look. I'd known I was going to catch some flak about the *Rumor Central* crew being here. I had shared a lot of people's secrets since my show started eight months ago and that had caused a whole lot of drama. I immediately went into the speech that I had worked on in my head the entire plane ride here.

"Look, we're about to have a blast." I pointed at the party bus. "That's compliments of *Rumor Central*. And wait until you see the room they got us." I figured if I could win over Kennedi and Sheridan, who were staying in the suite with me, they'd be more likely to convince the others that this wasn't such a bad idea. "I just have to film a little somethin' for the show. But you guys are straight."

"I don't care! No cameras!" this basketball player named Jock said after he bounced up next to Sheridan. "I'm 'bout to get into some mayhem and mischief up in Mexico. I don't need any documented proof. Matter of fact"—he took off his baseball hat and held it out toward us—"all of y'all, give me your iPhones and your Droids."

Of course, nobody paid him any attention, so he ended up putting his hat back on his head.

Evian stepped forward. She had her arms folded across her chest and was giving major attitude. She looked like she should be in some beach commercial with her butt-length hair pulled up into a loose ponytail and her Diane Von Furstenberg peach wrap dress. Evian's dad was a Persian billionaire, and so she always carried herself like some princess (although we'd heard lately that her family had some ties to the mafia).

"Mm-mm, Maya, this is so not cool," Evian said.

"For real," Shay said as she stepped up next to Evian. Shay should've been the poster child for ghetto royalty. Her thug-turned-NBA father was Jalen Turner, one of the hottest players in the NBA. Somebody should've told her that bleach-blond hair was so not a good look for black girls. Even now, she had on some Daisy Dukes shorts, a Run-D.M.C. tank top, and some high-top Converse. Just ghetto. Shay had been the saltiest about me getting my own show, but whatever.

"You're not about to blast our business all up over the world," Shay continued. "We all agreed that what happens in Cancun stays in Cancun."

"Yeah," Zenobia added. "And it can't stay in Mexico if you're catching it all on tape."

"It's not like you guys aren't going to be recording and posting stuff on Instagram anyway," I snapped back.

Quincy just stood there like he was enjoying the show.

"Look, you guys," I said, trying a different approach to calm everyone down. "I would've preferred that they didn't come either, but they're here and I didn't have a say-so in it, but what I did get them to agree to is a cut-off time. So anything that's scandalous in Cancun *will* stay here. I promise."

I didn't know how good I would make on that promise, but at this point, I needed to do my job and I didn't need the drama.

"And besides," I continued, "I did get them to agree to give me final say on whatever they air." I didn't really, but I needed to make them feel at ease.

"Oh yeah, because we know your judgment is on point," Shay said, rolling her eyes.

I gave her the hand and turned back to Sheridan and Kennedi. "All I'm saying is this is our chance to show the world how we party, diva style."

"I don't need anyone seeing me toasted," some girl from the back yelled.

I wanted to tell her she had nothing to worry about because the camera would *not* be pointed in her direction at all with her busted-looking self. But I ignored her.

"Doesn't matter to me," Kennedi finally said from the bus. Of course she'd be cool with it. Kennedi had my back all of the time, no matter what.

"I don't know, Maya. I'm not feeling this at all," Sheridan said, shaking her head. I didn't know why she was trippin' anyway. It's not like she'd be doing anything TV worthy anyway with her boring self. Sheridan was making me mad, though, because considering we were BFFs, she could be so shady sometimes.

"Just trust me," I said.

"Yeah, like that would ever happen," Shay mumbled as she turned and walked away.

Kennedi slid her sunglasses on. "Whatever. Just can we roll? I'm ready to get my party on."

I looked at Sheridan, waiting for a sign from her that she was cool with everything. Finally, she smiled and said, "Fine."

I nodded toward Quincy. "All right. I'll catch up with you later."

"Cool. Later." Quincy didn't say anything else as he made his way over to their waiting taxi.

"You foul," Jock said, wagging a finger at me. "But since you got this bus"—he broke out in a huge grin—"I forgive you." He jumped on the bus. "Let's get this party started!"

His silliness was just enough to get everybody back in party mode as they pushed any reservations aside. I just hoped that it stayed that way.

Chapter 3

The InterContinental Presidente penthouse was off the chain. I had already upgraded to a suite for me and my girls before I found out that Tamara wanted *Rumor Central* to film, but nothing could compare to this.

"Now *this* is how a diva is supposed to rock it," Sheridan said, tossing her purse onto the Italian leather sofa. She sure seemed okay with things now. She'd already claimed her bedroom. I pushed aside my thoughts. Sheridan was just being Sheridan. There was no sense in me tripping.

"Oh, it's about to be on!" Kennedi said, doing a slow twirl around the room just as Jock stuck his head in the door.

"Man," he said. "Sweet!" He invited himself in and started looking around. "I know where the party's going to be tonight."

"If you're lucky, you'll get invited," I said, joking. I really hadn't planned on having a full-fledged party, but the way this suite was set up, that seemed like a no-brainer.

"Oh, I'm inviting myself." Jock was the class clown so he kept everyone in stitches. He could be too silly sometimes, but he was always fun to be around. Jock plopped down on the sofa. "I hope the minibar is stocked 'cause your boy is ready to party."

I heard several other people coming down the hall and I looked up to see several more of my classmates, who all began piling in like I had a PARTY OVER HERE sign hanging on the door.

"Dang, can we get settled in first?" Sheridan said.

"Hey, we heard you guys were rocking the penthouse, so we came to see! Sweet," someone said as they walked in.

"Dang, can I be like you when I grow up?" Zenobia said, running her finger over the porcelain lamp sitting on the end table.

"How did you get this?" Evian said. I knew she would be on the phone to her daddy right away, trying to get him to buy the hotel or something so she could get a suite like this.

I wanted to tell Evian that green (with envy) wasn't her color. Instead, I just flashed a huge smile. "Top of the line, baby! Only top of the line for Maya Morgan. And you know we're gonna be throwing down." I walked over to the door, held it open, and said, "But for now we need to get changed and hit the beach, so can you guys exit to the left?" I motioned out into the hallway.

People started groaning and grumbling as they filed out. I was just about to say something to Jock, who hadn't moved off the sofa, when I saw my ex, Bryce, and his skanky new girlfriend, Callie, walking down the hall in front of my suite, holding hands.

Bryce was my first true love, a rich athlete with the swag of Chris Brown, the looks of Drake, and the fun-loving personality of Nick Cannon. I used to think that Bryce was the love of my life—until he played me for crazy and turned his back on me when he *thought* I did him wrong. I didn't have two words for Bryce now. He and his D-list girlfriend could have each other.

"What are you guys doing in there?" Bryce said to Zenobia as she exited.

"Whatever it is, *you* won't be doing it," I replied.

Callie turned her nose up when she noticed me. As if I really cared. "Nobody was talking to you," she said.

"I'm not trying to be around you, Maya," Bryce said, leaning in to peek in the suite.

"Good, then you'll get your nose out of my room," I snapped as I put my hand on his chest to push him back.

"Oh, this is your room?" Bryce said.

"It's my *suite*, because that's how I roll," I said with major attitude. Bryce made me so sick. He was the first guy I'd truly loved and the way he'd done me was just foul. Although I would never let him know, I still wasn't over it.

Just then, Jock approached the door. "Guess I'm out," he said. "For now."

"Okay, Jock," I said, squeezing his arm, trying my best to make Bryce jealous. "I'm going to see you back for the party tonight, though, right?"

"You can see me for the party right now. We can make our own party," Jock said, wiggling his hips in my direction.

I saw the veins in Bryce's neck stand up and I knew right away that Bryce was jealous as all get out. And even though we were no longer a couple, and it seemed like he had moved on, I could tell he couldn't stand to see me flirt with other guys. But then again, I was Maya Morgan, so that was understandable.

"Well, I need to get changed first," I said. "Maybe we'll have a private party later on."

"That's what I'm talking 'bout, baby, baby!" He walked out the door. "Who's the man?" he told his boys as they followed behind him. They all laughed.

Bryce had the nerve to lean in to me and whisper, "Desperation is so not becoming on you."

I stepped back and said, "Callie, can you get your man? Tell him don't worry about who I'm dating."

Callie swung her fake twenty-six-inch hair over her shoulder, crossed her arms, and glared at him. "Yeah, Bryce, why you all worried about what she's doing?"

"I'm not," Bryce said.

"Whatever," she huffed. "Let's go." She turned and stomped away without waiting for a reply.

I smiled because I could tell that both of them now had attitudes. I didn't care. That just made this trip that much better. I was going to have the time of my life—and piss Bryce off in the process. It didn't get any better than that.

Thirty minutes later, we had all changed into our bathing suits and were now heading to the hotel's pool. I spotted the lounge chair where Bryce and Callie were. I wanted to make sure to sashay past them, flaunting my Christian Dior teeny bikini. I knew my body was banging and there was no way I'd be able to pass by Bryce without him salivating like a hungry dog.

"Are you guys ready to party?" Kennedi said.

"I was ready the minute I stepped off the plane," I said. We laughed as we headed over to the pool.

"This way," I said, pointing in the opposite direction that we were heading. "There are some seats right there."

Sheridan frowned, and then she noticed Bryce and smiled. "My girl! I know that's right!" Sheridan said.

We walked past him and as expected, Bryce stopped talking mid-sentence and watched me. All I heard was Callie say, "No, you didn't!"

Me and my girls busted out laughing, but before we could get to some seats, the most gorgeous guy I'd ever seen in my life approached us.

"Today has got to be my lucky day," he said, looking me

dead in my face. He had the lightest gray eyes I'd ever seen. His wavy hair was cut just short enough and he had a body that was out of this world, which he had on full display since he was wearing only a pair of sagging swim trunks.

"You can't come up with a better line than that?" Kennedi said, raising an eyebrow.

"I'm not trying to come up with a line," he said, not taking his eyes off me. He took my hand and slowly kissed it. "Because when you see something this fine, you're literally speechless."

"Oh, give me a break," Kennedi said. She was always the skeptical one of the group, but I actually found this guy's flirting kind of cute.

"I'm Carson," he said extending his hand only at me. "Carson Wells."

Sheridan stepped in front of me before I could shake his hand. "Carson, is she the only one that you see?

"No disrespect," he said, still not taking his eyes off of me. "But she's the only one that matters."

"Pow," I said, laughing as I pushed Sheridan aside. I liked Carson already. "You have good taste, Carson."

"Tell me something I don't know," he said.

"Oh, and he's cocky," Kennedi said.

Carson didn't seem fazed as he kept talking. "What's your name, baby?" he asked me.

"It's not baby," I replied.

He smiled. His teeth could use a good whitening, but it was still one of the most beautiful smiles I'd ever seen. "My bad."

"The name is Maya," I said, deciding to hold off giving him my whole name. I *was* known worldwide now, after all.

"Umph, you here on Spring Break?" Kennedi asked, quizzing him.

"Yeah, I'm here with my school from Fulton County in Atlanta."

Kennedi gave him the once-over like she wasn't sure if she should believe him.

"So, what are you ladies about to get into?" he asked.

"You tell us," I said.

He took my hand again. "Why don't you come up to our cabana?" He pointed to a cabana in the corner of the pool area, overlooking the beach.

"I think I'd like that, but I don't know you like that, so my girls have to come with me," I replied.

"Oh, trust and believe, I have plenty of friends who'd love to entertain your girls while I get to know you better," he replied.

We giggled. This trip was definitely off to a good start, and when I saw the way Bryce was fuming, I knew it was only about to get better.

Chapter 4

Day one of Cancun fun was just kicking off and I was already having an awesome time. We'd hung out at Carson's cabana with him and his friends all day. Carson was a jokester and had kept us laughing all afternoon. Now, we were getting ready to go to a party.

I surveyed myself in the full-length mirror in the suite, admiring the Versace mini dress that stopped in the middle of my thighs. Not too high to be trashy and sexy enough to be classy. I had just fluffed out my curls when the phone in my hotel room rang. It was probably Carson telling me to hurry up. He'd called me a few hours ago to invite me and my girls down to the party. I was supposed to meet him thirty minutes ago, but he needed to understand that beauty took time.

I smiled as I answered, ready to get my flirt on. "Hello?"

"Maya."

I groaned at the sound of my boss's voice. "Hey, Tamara."

"Don't sound so happy to hear from me," she said.

"No, I should've known. I thought you'd at least give me one day here before you were calling to check in." I leaned into the mirror and applied some more lip gloss.

"Now you know me better than that," Tamara replied. I could just picture her at her desk, looking all clean in her designer suit as she sifted through papers. Tamara was the queen of multitasking. "So, how's it going?"

"We just got here, Tamara," I said.

"Well, what do you have lined up for us? We're looking forward to seeing what you come back with."

I rolled my eyes. "Well, I'm just going to see how things play out." I knew that I needed to start digging, but dang, could I enjoy myself for just a little while?

I could hear the frustration in Tamara's voice. "Maya, I need to stress to you how important this is. This is our first time taking this show on the road. The next trip they're talking about is to Aruba. Wouldn't you love to take *Rumor Central* to Aruba?"

Oh yes, I thought. That would definitely be the business.

"But the only way that's going to work," Tamara continued, "is if you prove that this whole 'on the road with *Rumor Central*' trip is worth it. And the way to prove that is by coming back with something worth covering, some sizzling stories."

"Yeah, yeah, yeah, I got it."

Her tone changed, obviously trying to lighten the mood. "So, where are you guys going tonight?" Tamara asked.

"Well, Diddy's son Justin is here and he's having a party at a hotel, so we're going over there."

"Oooh," she said. I could just see her eyes dancing all excitedly. "That should be good. I'm sure that's going to be a star-studded event, so you should be able to get something. Okay, I'll let you go because you probably need to get rolling. Marcus is your undercover guy. He arrived this morning. So you should be all set."

I couldn't help it. I had to appeal to her one last time.

"Tamara, you know I'm going to try and get you some dirt, but just so you know, my friends are so not going to be feeling this. They are not going to give Quincy anything worth filming."

"That's why we sent two cameramen and the spy cam. Quincy can get the regular stuff on the air and then Marcus can use the little spy cam to get all the good stuff later on. You just tell everyone Marcus is an old friend or something if they ask why he's hanging around."

I really didn't like going behind my friends' backs and taping them like that, but I knew that was my job. I just made a mental note that I would cut out anything that would get any of my closest friends in trouble. Everyone else was fair game.

"Cool, I'm all over it," I said.

"I sure hope so, Maya. We're counting on you."

We said our good-byes, and I took one last look in the mirror before getting Sheridan and Kennedi and heading downstairs.

We made our way across the street to where the party was.

"About time," Carson said, smiling as he greeted us.

"Beauty takes time," I replied.

He looked me up and down, his eyes giving his approval. "And you are beautiful." He took my hand. "Come on."

Inside the hotel's club, the party was in full effect. There were hot-bodied young people of every race and nationality. It was like a freakin' United Nations party.

Justin definitely knew how to party. The music was pumping and everyone was having a blast. And of course, I was enjoying the VIP section along with my friends.

Around eleven o'clock, the *policia*, what they called the cops in Cancun, came in and shut the party down. It was just too many people, and hotel guests were complaining. It looked like our party was over.

As we made our way outside with all of the other disgruntled party people, Carson said, "You know it's too early to go back the hotel. Let's take this party to the beach."

"Oh, I'm definitely feeling that," Kennedi said.

"Yeah, a couple of my friends are already there," Carson said.

"They got the brews and we've got the broads," one of Carson's friends added.

I looked at him like he was crazy. "Broads?" I said.

"You'll have to excuse Jeremy—he has no class," Carson said.

I rolled my eyes at Jeremy, but we still went ahead and followed Carson out. Kennedi, Sheridan, Shay, Evian, and a few other girls also followed us out. I wanted to know why Evian and Shay were coming, but I'd noticed earlier how Shay had hooked up with Carson's friend Princeton.

The party on the beach was nothing like the one we had just left, but it was still fun. We were laughing and telling jokes and just having a good time. A few folks were buzzed, but no one was out of order—yet. Finally, Carson said, "Anybody up for a game?"

"What kind of game?" I asked.

"Truth or dare," he replied, a sneaky grin on his face.

"Really? Truth or dare?" Sheridan said. "Isn't that so seventh grade?"

Carson and his friend exchanged glances. "Not the way we play it," Princeton said.

"And just how do you play it?" Shay asked, as she leaned back on Princeton like she was his girl.

"No, this is grown-folks truth or dare," Carson said.

I glanced over at Marcus, the undercover cameraman who had the spy cam glasses on. He had slowly eased out with us. When Carson asked me who he was, I'd lied and said one of our classmates. I was sure he was getting everything on video. Marcus was perfect playing that role because he looked like he couldn't be more than seventeen.

I gave Marcus the signal we'd agreed upon to let him know this was definitely something he needed to start filming. His glasses were going to record our escapades in high definition.

Carson explained the rules. It was about twenty of us sitting around.

"I'll start," one of the girls I didn't know said. She turned to Princeton. "So, I dare you to take off your underwear and go skinny-dipping in the ocean."

"Really?" he said, standing up as he stepped out of his clothes—all of them. "Is that the best you've got?" He laughed as he took off into the water.

Shay looked disgusted behind it all. I and everyone else actually thought it was funny as we watched his wrinkly booty take off running.

"His butt looks like a prune!" someone yelled, and we all busted out laughing, everyone except for Shay.

A few minutes later, Princeton emerged, dripping wet and butt naked. He stood in front of the crowd, all of his privates boldly on display. "My turn!" he announced.

"Yeah, can you put your drawers on?" Sheridan said as we all kept laughing.

Shay tossed Princeton his underwear and he stepped back in them, then looked around and said, "Let me see. Who's next? You!" He pointed at me. "I dare you to flash your breasts."

This fool had straight lost his mind. "Sweetie, these are only reserved for certain people."

"Come on," Carson said, trying to coax me as he scooted closer. "You know how the game is played."

"No. I don't get down like that," I said.

"Don't punk out, Maya," Kennedi said. I know she was teasing me because she of all people knew that wasn't about to happen.

"The only way out is if someone takes your turn," Carson said.

Suddenly one of the quiet girls who had been sitting off to the side said, "I'll take her turn." Before anyone knew it, she had pulled her shirt up and flashed her breasts.

"Ewww!" Sheridan exclaimed.

"Wow!" several of the guys said as they began whooping and hollering.

All I did was shake my head. *Incredibly tacky.*

"Now it's my turn." The girl pointed at Carson. "I dare you"—she pulled a dollar out of her pocket—"to put this dollar inside *her* underwear." She pointed to the redheaded girl next to her and I could tell by the way the girl was giggling they had planned this. *How incredibly lame.* But Carson was up to the challenge because he stepped up.

"My pleasure," he said, taking the dollar.

The crowd started shouting, "Make it rain," as the redheaded girl stood and did a stripper dance. Carson put the dollar in his mouth, then leaned in and placed the money in her underwear. Yeah, he had just lost major cool points with me on that move.

Carson must've known I wasn't feeling that move because after he finished, he turned and said, "I'm gonna let my princess here take my turn." He flashed an apologetic smile.

I decided not to trip and instead looked around our group until my eyes settled on Evian. "I dare you to hook up with a random guy," I said to her.

"What?" Evian said.

"I didn't stutter," I said. "I dare you to go meet up with a random guy."

"I'm not doing that," she said, her nose turned up. The shocked look on her face was actually funny, like she was too good for something like that.

"Un-unh, you gotta do it," Carson said. "Those are the rules."

"Why you trying to break the rules, Evian? You scared?" I asked. I knew Evian was prissy. She had that old money and was always looking at stuff like it was beneath her.

"I know you're not talking," Evian snapped. "You just passed on your dare."

"That's the way the game is played." I shrugged. "Get somebody to take your turn and you can pass, too."

She looked around. No one said a word.

"No takers, so you have to go," I said, teasing her. "But if you just scared and want to punk out the game, don't do it."

"And just what am I supposed to do with this random guy? Where am I supposed to find him?" Evian asked, looking around.

I looked to Carson for help. He glanced around also, paused, then pointed up to a guy sitting up the hill at a bar.

"Princeton, go get that guy in the red hat."

Without asking another question, Princeton jumped up and ran up the hill.

We continued to tease Evian about bailing out of the game when she again said she didn't want to do it.

When the guy returned, he said, "What's up? Someone wanted to see me?"

They couldn't have picked a plainer guy. He had on some plaid Bermuda shorts and a raggedy Coke T-shirt. There was absolutely nothing cute about his frazzled-looking hair and pimply face. He looked like a creepy old tourist.

Carson spoke up. "Hey, man, we're playing a little game here and Evian—isn't that your name?"

She didn't reply, but I said, "Yes, that's her name."

Carson turned back to the guy, a huge grin on his face. "Evian is going to take a little stroll with you," he said.

The guy raised an eyebrow and said, "A stroll where?"

"Wherever you'd like to go," Carson replied.

The guy looked at Evian and dang near salivated at the mouth. "And what are we going to do on this stroll?"

"That's up to you and her," Carson said, patting him on the back.

"We're not going to do anything," Evian said, although she did stand up. "I'll take the stupid stroll, but that's it."

The guy grinned like he couldn't believe his luck. "Are you going to at least talk to me?" he asked.

"Just come on," she said, taking his hand and pulling him away. She stopped and turned to Carson. "Where are we supposed to stroll anyway?"

"You have to at least walk to the gazebo on the next hotel's property and back," Carson announced.

"That's a long way," Evian moaned. "This game is so stupid."

"Hey, my game, my rules." Carson threw his hands up.

"Fine, whatever." Evian rolled her eyes as she stomped away.

"Thanks, man," the guy said, scurrying after Evian. He fell in the sand as he tried to catch up with her. But he quickly pulled himself up and scrambled to catch up. We all laughed like crazy. We would never let Evian live this down.

We did a few more dares, but after a while, most of us were getting bored.

"This game is dumb," Sheridan declared.

"Yeah, I'm bored with it, too," someone else said.

"Let's get out of here," Princeton told Shay.

"I need to wait on Evian," she replied.

"Well, at least let's go up to the bar," he pleaded. Shay shrugged, then let him help her up to go to the bar.

Carson's other friend, Damien, turned to Kennedi. "Hey, pretty lady, can me and my friend buy you and your girl some drinks, too?" he asked, motioning toward Sheridan.

Both of them looked at me. Then Sheridan said, "Why don't we all go up to the bar."

"Naw, you guys go on," Carson said, pulling me closer. "I have something I'd rather be doing anyway."

He looked at me, licking his lips. He just didn't know.

That little dollar-bill trick had just cost him the chance to get to know Maya Morgan.

"No, I'm coming, too." I tried to break free from his grip.

Carson wouldn't let go of my hand. "Then, we're all going to the bar." He flashed a smile at me. "I see I rubbed someone the wrong way and I've got some making up to do."

Damien didn't wait for them to reply as he grabbed Kennedi's hand and pulled her. "Come on, ladies. Drinks are on me!"

Chapter 5

So, Carson had redeemed himself and I was actually having a good time. Damien was keeping us entertained at the bar with his impressions of the hottest movie stars. This boy was good, and I definitely could see him on the big screen one day.

Shay had even been cool, laughing and cracking up at Damien's impressions. Finally, she glanced at her watch. "Hey, shouldn't Evian be back by now?"

I looked at my cell phone as well, since no one else seemed concerned. The guys were taking shots. And a couple of girls were hanging right along with them. I was the only one not really drinking. I wasn't a prude, but I couldn't stand the yucky way liquor made me feel so I stuck to my Shirley Temple. Besides, I never needed anything taking me off my A game. Everyone else, though, was getting hammered. Even Kennedi was giggling like some second-grader and Sheridan was asleep with her head on the bar, after only one drink.

"They've only been gone about an hour," I said.

"Yeah, but . . ." Shay shook her head like she was seriously worried. I couldn't understand how she and Evian had gotten to be so close. They couldn't be more different. Shay was an around-the-way, new-money girl, and Evian was an old-money princess type.

"But nothing. Y'all are forgetting where you are," Carson said, sliding back over to me. He was buzzed but nothing too bad. "You're in Cancun," he continued. "It's all about a good time. I guarantee you ol' girl decided to hook up with that guy. They probably got to talkin' and now she's off doing her own thing and you guys are worried about where she is."

"He was so not Evian's type," Shay said.

I definitely wasn't stressing over Evian of all people, but that was a little strange that she would be gone that long with a random dude. I'd seen Marcus follow Evian, so I decided to go call him.

"Excuse me," I said, standing up. "I need to make a call."

"Who are you calling in Cancun?" Kennedi asked.

"Yeah, do you have any idea how much that's gonna cost?" Damien said, his voice slurred.

"Sweetie, when you're Maya Morgan you don't worry about roaming charges and long-distance charges."

"That's what I'm talking about," Carson said as I walked off.

I eased off to the side of the bar and punched in Marcus's number. His voice mail picked up. "Hey, Marcus," I said, leaving a message. "Where are you? Call me and let me know what's up. Evian hasn't gotten back yet and I was just wondering where she went."

I had just hung up the phone when I saw Marcus inside the hotel at the bar, flirting with someone.

I swung open the hotel door and marched over to him. "Marcus?"

"Oh hey, Maya, what's up?" He looked up with a big, cheesy grin across his face as he set his drink down on the bar. Some woman with her boobs hanging out of a teeny bikini was latched onto his arm.

"What are you doing?" I asked.

He motioned toward the woman, who did a little shimmy.

"What does it look like I'm doing? I'm about to have a little fun in Cancun myself."

"Excuse me, we're supposed to be working," I said in a shushed tone so the woman wouldn't be all up in our business.

"Not around the clock. And correct me if I'm wrong, but aren't you out there kickin' it with your friends? I'm entitled to a little fun, too."

"Yeah, but you were supposed to be getting video of Evian and that guy." I shook my head in frustration. My other cameraman, Quincy, would've never done this.

"And I did get video."

"Okay, so where are they?" I asked.

"I don't know," he said, the expression on his face wondering why I was even questioning him. "Look, you told me to get video of them. That's what I did. It was actually quite boring because they were just walking and talking, so I got some video and when they went in the hotel, I bounced."

"What do you mean when they went in the hotel?"

"Just what I said. They went in the hotel." He pointed toward the front door. "The one across the street. Probably to get their freak on."

"Yeah, like we are trying to do," the woman said, giggling as she leaned in to stick her nasty tongue in his ear.

Tramp.

Marcus licked his lips at her then turned back to me. "So, look here, I did what you needed me to do. I'm off the clock. If your girl hasn't returned, then chances are she's up in ol' boy's room doing what I'm trying to do."

"Ugh!" I rolled my eyes and stomped off.

I couldn't be completely mad because Marcus had made it clear that he planned to enjoy himself while he was here. But that was still messed up for Marcus to just leave her like that.

"Where have you been?" Kennedi asked once I went

back outside. No one knew that Marcus was an undercover cameraman, so I couldn't say anything, not even to my BFFs.

"I just went to go check on something." I glanced around, hoping Evian had returned while I was gone. "So Evian still hasn't made it back?"

"No," Shay said.

Sheridan finally raised her head. Her eyes were bloodshot, but she did manage to say, "I knew this game was stupid. You guys sending her off with some strange guy."

"I didn't send her anywhere," the girl who flashed her breasts said. "I don't even know that chick. Come on, Crystal." She motioned for her friend and they got up and left.

"Would you girls chill?" Carson said. "It's not too far she could've gone. I guarantee you she's somewhere kickin' it and you guys are all up in her business."

"Fine," I said.

"It's your fault she went off anyway," Shay said, appearing next to Carson.

"*My* fault? I didn't put a gun to her head and make her do anything," I told Shay.

"Whatever."

"Look, I'm tired of all of this bickering. We are supposed to be having fun," Kennedi said. "All this fighting is blowing my buzz."

"I think I'm gonna be sick," Sheridan moaned, grabbing her stomach.

"Come on, I'll take you back to the room," I told her. See, this was exactly why I didn't get drunk. Now, Sheridan was all sick and stuff. Who wanted that?

"I'm just gonna stay . . ." She leaned over the barstool and threw up everywhere.

"Uggh!" several people shouted as they jumped out of the way.

I was beyond disgusted, but I walked to one side to help her up. Kennedi went to the other. I almost dropped her because I jumped out the way as she got ready to throw up again.

Carson caught her before she hit the ground. "Come on. I got you. I'll help you back to your room."

I was grateful because I didn't do vomit. Just as we were about to leave, Shay said, "So wait, you guys are just going to leave before Evian gets back?"

"Evian isn't our responsibility," Kennedi said.

"That's foul. But foul needs to be your middle name," Shay told me. "And I guess birds of a feather," she added, turning her nose up at Sheridan and Kennedi.

"Whatever." I turned to Carson. "Let's get her back to the room and in the bed." We headed inside and left Shay and Princeton at the bar. She could sit there all night and wait on Evian for all I cared. My awesome night had ended in a bust.

Chapter 6

I knew I should've followed my gut and just stayed in the room when we put Sheridan to bed. But I'd let Carson convince me to take a walk with him on the beach. Kennedi had passed out right along with Sheridan. As the only one who wasn't drunk, I wasn't sleepy, so I hadn't been ready for bed. I think that's the only reason I gave in.

But we hadn't been walking for ten minutes before I started feeling like this had been a bad idea. Now, I knew without a doubt that it was. Carson had had way too much to drink. And everything I'd found charming about him just a few hours ago was getting on my last nerve.

"So, you know I'm feeling you," he said, walking as he kept trying to put his arm around me. There were a few other couples walking along the beach and a few frolicking in the water, but other than that, the beach was deserted, which was kind of shocking since it was only around two in the morning.

I removed his arm for the fifteenth time. "You know, you don't know me well enough to know if you're feeling me or not."

"But you're beautiful and . . ." He stepped back and looked

me up and down like some kind of old creep. ". . . and fine as all get out."

I don't know what I ever saw in him. Yes, he was cute. But that was it. They say liquor brings out the true person. I was glad that I had seen it in Carson so now I didn't have to waste any more of my trip with him.

"Well, I think I'm going to get on back," I said.

"Why are you trippin'? You acting all stuck up and everything. It's just me and you. Your girls are out for the night." Carson stepped closer to me. "We up under the Mexico moonlight and need to take advantage of it." Then, this fool actually tried to lean in and suck on my neck. Disgusting!

"Ugh," I said, stepping out of his way. "Personal space? You're all up in it!"

"Come on, lil mama. Let's go back to my room."

I pushed him away. Harder this time. "First of all, I'm not a *lil mama* and second of all, I don't know you like that."

"Well, you can get to know me," he said, laughing as he tried to pull me into a bear hug. His breath stank from all the liquor he'd been drinking.

"Get up off of me!" I said, pushing him back.

"Oh, so now you gon' be some kind of stuck-up skank?"

"I got your stuck-up skank!" I snapped. I took a deep breath. I didn't need to be getting upset over this buster. "You know what, I'm going back to my room," I said, pushing him out of my way. I couldn't stand thirsty guys, and Carson was acting like he was straight dehydrated.

He lost his smile and pointed a finger in my face. "Look, I don't like girls that try to be teases."

His whole tone was out of order and I was so done. "Yeah, and on that note, I'm out," I said. I turned and walked away. Enough of trying to be nice to him. He could fall out sloppy drunk for all I cared. I was done with him. Maya Morgan didn't do thirsty, and she dang sure didn't do sloppy drunk and rude.

"Come here, girl. This ain't over." He reached out and grabbed my arm. "Do you know I coulda had any pick of the chicks out here?"

I looked at his hand on my arm, then up at him, then back at his hand. Then, I gently removed his hand. "Well, that's good to know. Now go pick up somebody else," I said.

I turned and walked away again. This time, he grabbed my arm a lot harder. "I said, you ain't going nowhere."

"Hey! Have you lost your mind?" I said, jerking away from him.

He snatched me toward him, then flung me to the ground. I felt sand creeping all up in my back. I screamed just as he jumped on top of me and covered my mouth.

"Lil uppity slut! I'm not playin' with you! You not gonna sit here and have me wasting all my time!"

"Get off of me," I tried to scream as I hit at him. I didn't know what he was about to do, but I knew that whatever it was, he was going to have to kill me to get it done because although I wasn't a fighter, I was about to go straight Laila Ali on him. I hit him with everything I could, but it wasn't enough. His strength overpowered me, and it felt like I wasn't making any progress. In fact, it seemed like my fighting was only making him angrier. I was just about to try and knee him in his groin when I heard him scream as someone yanked him off of me.

"Get off of her!" the voice said. I looked up to see Bryce pulling Carson away. He flung Carson to the ground and then immediately jumped on him and started hitting him in the face. "You want to manhandle somebody? Manhandle me!" Bryce said as he pummeled Carson.

I scurried up, and it was then that I noticed Callie standing there in shock.

"Bryce, stop!" Callie screamed, reaching over and pulling at his arm. "Stop before you hurt him!"

Hurt *him?* I wanted to say. This fool was trying to rape me and she was worried about Bryce hurting him?

"Let me go," Bryce said, jerking away from Callie. But it was enough of a distraction for Carson to jump up and take off running.

"Come back here, you punk!" Bryce yelled after him.

By that point, I had pulled myself off the ground and was struggling not to cry. I'd been accosted once before, by some deranged stalker in the mall, but I'd never come this close to being seriously attacked, especially by someone I was on a date with.

"Are you okay?" Bryce asked, coming to my side. He lifted my chin and studied my face.

"Yeah, yeah, I'm all right," I said, trying to brush some of the sand off of me. "He was just drunk and completely trippin'."

"Who is that?" Bryce asked.

"I don't know." I shrugged. "Some guy from Atlanta that I was hanging out with."

Bryce gave me a chastising look, and for a moment our eyes met. I know we had fallen out, but he looked—I don't know, scared for me. We stood eyeing each other until Callie cleared her throat.

"Okay, Superman," she said. "You've saved the damsel in distress, so can we continue our romantic walk on the beach?"

I didn't even bother acknowledging her. She wasn't worth my eye space, so I simply told Bryce, "Thanks a lot. Who knows what that creep would've done."

"Where's Mann?" he asked, referring to my part-time bodyguard.

"At home. I wasn't trying to go on my spring break trip with my bodyguard."

He shook his head. "You know, with the show and all, you can't be running around with strange guys," Bryce said. I didn't know if he was saying that out of jealousy or concern, but either way, it brought a smile to my face.

"I know, I shouldn't have been out here, but don't worry. I'm a big girl. I can handle myself." Even as I said it, I thought about what could've happened if Bryce hadn't come along.

Again, Callie cleared her throat, not bothering to hide her attitude.

"So, where are you about to go?" Bryce asked.

"I'm trying to go back to my room."

Bryce said, "Why are you by yourself anyway? Where's your crew?"

"They're back in the room asleep. I was just . . ." Suddenly, I felt so stupid. "You know what? I'm cool. I'm just gonna go back to my room"

"You can't walk out here by yourself," he said.

I looked around the beach. Carson was gone, but who knew if he would come back. The few couples that were out were gone. "Yeah, I know." Normally, I would've played it all big and bad, but Carson really had me scared and I didn't want to be out here alone.

"We'll walk you back," Bryce announced.

Callie's head spun around like she was in a horror movie.

"We can't let her walk by herself," Bryce protested. "What if that creep comes back?"

"Really, Bryce?" she said.

"No, it's cool. I'll be all right." I wasn't in the mood for drama, and I was two seconds from telling Callie about herself.

"No," Bryce said like it wasn't up for discussion. "I wouldn't let you walk by yourself, Callie, and I'm not going to let her walk by herself. We'll just make sure she gets back okay, and then we can come back."

She kept her lips poked out and her arms folded, but I could tell by the determined look on Bryce's face that he didn't care. So, I couldn't help it. I leaned in, hugged Bryce, and said, "Thanks. You always come through for me." Then I smiled as he began leading me down the beach.

Chapter 7

I awoke to the sound of someone banging on my hotel room door. Kennedi and Sheridan were in the other bedrooms in the suite. All three of us got up and walked into the living area at the same time.

"What the . . . ?" Kennedi said, rubbing her eyes as she stumbled out of her room. Both she and Sheridan looked like they had been run over by eighteen-wheelers. I guess they were hung over. Yet another reason I didn't drink.

Sheridan yawned. "It's six in the morning. Somebody has lost their mind," she groaned.

"If this is housekeeping, they are going to get a piece of my mind," I said, stomping toward the door. "Who is it?" I snapped.

"It's Shay! Open the door!" she screamed.

"Shay?" I looked out the peephole and Shay was on the other side, looking frantic. "What?" I said, swinging the door open.

"Have you all heard from Evian?" she said.

"Why would we have heard from Evian?" Sheridan asked, appearing beside me.

"She still hasn't come back to the room."

"What?" I replied.

"Maybe it's like Carson said," Kennedi replied. "Maybe she's somewhere getting her freak on."

"Not with a total stranger," Shay said, brushing past us and into the room. "Evian doesn't get down like that. I'm worried and then you know the chaperones are going to come looking for her at breakfast."

"Please," I said. I wasn't about to stress over the chaperones. "They're trying to have a good time themselves. They aren't the least bit worried about us."

Shay started pacing back and forth across the living room. "This is serious, Maya. I'm worried that something has really happened to Evian. If she didn't come back to the room, that means she still has on the same clothes, she hasn't brushed her teeth or anything."

That actually made me pause because Evian was obsessive about her hygiene.

"Maybe she found a convenience store," Sheridan said. Even she was starting to look a little nervous.

"How could she when I have her purse?" Shay replied. She was shaking as she kept pacing. "You guys need to help me find her."

I looked at Shay like she was crazy. "It's six in the morning."

"I don't care what time it is," Shay said. "You guys need to come help me look."

"Why do we need to help you do anything?" I asked. It's not like Shay or Evian even liked me anyway, so I don't know why she thought I would drop everything to help.

Shay glared at me. "Because you were the one pushing her to play this stupid truth-or-dare game."

I blinked in shock. I hoped she wasn't about to try and blame Evian's disappearance on me. I hadn't put a gun to that girl's head and made her participate.

"Tell me this, Miss Superstar," Shay said, stepping toward me. "Have you ever heard of Natalee Holloway?"

That shut me up. Because I knew all about the girl who had gone missing in Aruba during her senior trip.

"Who is Natalee Holloway?" Sheridan asked.

Shay rolled her eyes like Sheridan was some kind of doofus. "The chick that went on her senior trip in Acapulco and was never seen again."

"It was Aruba," I said, correcting her.

"Whatever," Shay said, side-eying me. "My point is she came up missing!"

"Oh yeah, I remember that," Kennedi said. "Didn't they find her body or something? Some local dudes killed her?"

"Exactly," Shay said, turning back to me. "What if something happened to Evian? Do you want that on your conscience? You want your stupid show sued behind this?"

Of course I didn't, and I dang sure didn't want *Rumor Central* tied to any of this.

"I'm sure Evian is fine," I said.

"And you know this how?" Shay snapped. She seemed really agitated, like she'd been up all night worrying about Evian.

"What do you expect us to do?" Kennedi said.

"I don't know, go find your little boyfriend that hooked this stupid game up and make him help us," Shay responded.

"He's not my boyfriend. Matter of fact, I have nothing to say to him," I replied.

"Well, you'd better find something to say. We need to talk to him, or just go ask around to see if anybody has seen Evian. We need to go to the cops."

"Whoa," Kennedi said. "I don't do five-o, especially foreign five-o."

"I don't do my best friend getting killed, either," Shay said bluntly.

"Wh-who said anything about killed?" Sheridan stammered.

Shay inhaled deeply. "Okay, maybe I'm going a little overboard. I hope she's safe, but I'm not going to sit around and do nothing, and neither are you," she said, glaring at me.

"Look, I'm not in that," I protested.

Shay turned up her lip like she wasn't trying to hear me. "Yes, you are, and you're going to go in there and change out of your little silk pajamas or whatever else you need to do for your morning routine and let's go."

"Maya Morgan doesn't take orders," I said defiantly.

"You ain't the only one that can shine on TV," Shay said, stepping toward me. "Because I will be all on *The Today Show*, *Good Morning America*, and anybody else with a camera telling them how you pushed Evian into playing that stupid truth-or-dare game and how her disappearance is all on you. And then, after I finish my round of media interviews, I'm going to her mob family and letting them know that, too."

If Shay didn't have my attention before, she definitely had it now.

I looked over to Sheridan. Kennedi didn't know Evian like we did. But the look on Sheridan's face told me I didn't have a choice. I'd better get dressed and help Shay get to searching for Evian. Because if Evian didn't turn up . . . it wasn't going to be a pretty sight.

Chapter 8

"What are you doing?" Sheridan stood over me, her hands plastered on her hips.

I didn't budge as I replied. "What does it look like? I'm relaxing by the pool."

"I have been looking everywhere for you," Sheridan said. "I just went back up to the room to see if you were there."

"Okay, well now you found me." I turned over on my stomach, letting the rays hit my face. "What's up?"

"Maya, why are you out here chillin'?"

I was lying in one of the lounge chairs by the pool, and finally getting a chance to just relax, so I couldn't appreciate having that relaxation interrupted. I blew a frustrated breath, then sat up on the lounge chair. "Um, isn't that what we came to Cancun for?" I asked her.

"You told Shay you were going to go look for Evian some more."

I was too through. We'd looked everywhere this morning. We even missed our senior breakfast as we traipsed all over the place trying to track her down. Not to mention the fact that Shay had even stuffed pillows under the covers so when the chaperones checked on them this morning, they'd think Evian was still asleep. Finally, by noon, I was done. I went back to the room, ordered room service, ate, then changed. Now, I was spending the rest of the day taking my cue from Kennedi and just chilling.

"And I did look for her some more. And I didn't find her." Granted, I'd looked on my way down the elevator from the penthouse floor, and then, on my way to the pool. But I'd still looked. Besides, earlier, I'd left a message for Carson, walked down to the beach, looked around, and still saw no sign of Evian so I had done my part. "Evian is not about to ruin my trip."

It was at that moment that Kennedi strolled over as well. She had been lying out with me and had gone to get something to drink. She didn't say a word as she pulled her lounge chair out and laid back down in it. I actually was under a shaded umbrella because while I was enjoying the heat, I wasn't trying to tan. Kennedi who was light as all get out, welcomed the sun. But my perfectly chocolaty skin was fine just as it was.

"We went and looked for her, what else are we supposed to do? Ruin our whole trip behind that girl?" I asked. "She's probably off laid up with dude somewhere."

"Maya, do I need to remind you of how serious this could be?" Sheridan was starting to sound like somebody's mama. A total drag.

"Yeah, yeah, I know, the whole Natalee Holloway thing." I sat up. "But that's not what this is. Evian tries to fool everybody into thinking she's some kind of Goody Two-shoes, but remember, she was the one behind the whole little prostitution ring at Miami High. So she's not as innocent as everyone thinks. She's probably off somewhere just like Carson said, enjoying herself and getting her freak on. She'll turn up today."

"You'd better hope so," Sheridan said, shaking her head doubtfully. "Because I was thinking about what Shay said, and

I think she's right. You could be held liable for her disappearance."

That made me sit up all the way and remove my glasses. "Me? I wish you guys would quit saying that. Why would I be responsible? I didn't do anything to her."

Sheridan shook her head like I wasn't getting it. "Yeah, but you're the one that pushed her to go off with that guy and tons of people saw it."

"So? I didn't make her go." I turned up my nose. I had no idea why everyone kept trying to drag me into this.

"And whose side are you on anyway, Sheridan?" Kennedi finally spoke up.

"Maya's, of course." She turned back to me and pointed a warning finger. "You remember that case in Arizona? The girls were charged and sent to prison because they taunted one of their classmates until she jumped off a bridge. They didn't push her. They didn't force her to jump. They just teased her and taunted her until she jumped. They were charged and are now in jail."

"First of all," I replied, pointing a finger right back. "My dad would have attorneys all over that, so I'm not the least bit worried about jail." I didn't know if she was trying to scare me or what, but Sheridan, of all people, should know I'm not the one.

"Well, you should be worried because even if your dad gets you off, do you really want to go through a trial? And do you really want to be all up in the news with Evian's family blaming you? Evian's *mafia* family?"

Now here Sheridan went talking about that mafia mess. But she had a point. I needed to be reminded that Evian's family was bona fide crazy.

"You really think they would blame me?" I asked.

"Let something happen to their little princess, of course I do," she replied.

I threw up my hands. This whole thing made me wish

that I had never met Evian Javid. "I don't' know what I'm supposed to do."

"You need to do like Shay said and go do some digging. That's what you do, right? Go talk to Carson. Find out if he knows anything about that guy. Go to the hotel they were last seen at. You can't just walk around here"—she motioned wildly around the pool area—"calling Evian's name and then say 'oh, well, I couldn't find her.' If something has happened to Evian, you could be held liable and you don't need the drama."

Sheridan knew me well because that was exactly what I had done.

"Ugh," I groaned as I sat up. I couldn't believe my vacation was being ruined by this foolishness. "Fine."

Kennedi sat up. "Where are you going?"

I wrapped my skirt around my bottom. "I think Carson told me where he was staying so I'm gonna go talk to him."

"Well, good luck with that," Kennedi said, lying back down.

"Thanks a lot, *friend*," I told her.

Kennedi gave me a back-handed wave. "Anytime," she said as she flipped over.

"Come on," I told Sheridan. "I'm going to go change and then we can go look for this girl. And when I find her, I'm going to give her a piece of my mind for messing up my vacation like this."

"*If* we find her," Sheridan said.

"Will you stop being so negative? We're going to find her, and *when* we find her, I'm going to cuss her little slutty behind out."

I put my shades on and sashayed toward the elevator, hoping that this didn't take too long so I could come back and relax by the pool.

Chapter 9

This was not the way I had planned to spend my day.

"Which one is it?" Sheridan said.

I could tell she was irritated, but shoot, so was I. "I don't know," I said, looking at the two hotels. "I just remember it's one of these. I can't remember the name, but he said he was staying at the hotel on the corner of Eldorado and Caprica. So we'll just check both hotels."

"Like they're really going to give you information on a hotel guest," she said, jumping out of the way just as a bicyclist almost ran her over.

"Girl, this is Cancun, they don't have the same kind of regulations."

"This is ridiculous," she muttered.

"You're the one that insisted we do this, so come on!" I said, pulling her toward the first hotel. We went inside and I marched straight up to the front desk. "Hi, I'm looking for a Carson Wells."

"Do you know what room he's in?" the clerk asked, as she began tapping some keys on her computer.

"No, I don't," I said. "Can you just look and see if you have a guest by that name?"

The front desk clerk continued tapping away on the computer, and I gave Sheridan the eye to say, *See, I told you.*

"I'm sorry, we don't have a guest here by that name," the clerk said.

I frowned. "Are you sure?"

"I'm positive."

I hesitated, thinking, then said, "Okay, are the kids from Fulton County in Atlanta here?"

"No, we don't have any of the spring breakers here," the woman said. "We were booked for a technology conference."

"Okay. Thank you," I said, grabbing Sheridan's hand and making my way back out. "Let's go across the street and check out the other hotel. It has to be that one."

Sheridan reluctantly followed me and we repeated the scenario. I stood at the desk as the clerk tapped away. "Sorry, we don't have a Carson Wells here."

"What?" I said. "No, but he has to be here. This has to be the hotel." I looked around. "The one where he said he was staying. Is this where Fulton County students are, the kids from Atlanta?"

The woman clicked again. "Yep."

"Well, then, there." I tapped her computer. "Carson Wells, check again."

"I'm sorry, but we don't have anybody here by that name." She pointed to a tall, lanky man standing at the end of the counter. "Talk to that guy. He's one of the chaperones for the trip for students from Fulton County."

"Thank you," I said, quickly making my way down to the edge of the counter.

I tapped him on the shoulder. "Excuse me, sir."

"Yes, ma'am, how may I help you?" the man said, turning toward me.

"Yeah, I'm trying to find one of your students. You *are* from Fulton County, aren't you?"

The man nodded. "Yes."

"Well, I need to get in touch with one of your students."

He let out a loud sigh. You could tell the students had been working his nerves. "Who is it, and what did they do now?"

"Oh, no. It's not that at all," I said. "I just need to talk to him. It's very important."

"Well, who is it?" he repeated.

"Carson Wells," I said.

The man stopped and frowned. "Carson Wells? We don't have a student named Carson Wells."

Both Sheridan and I stood frozen. Finally I said, "Excuse me? Yes, you do."

"No," he said slowly, his eyes going up in his head like he was thinking. "I'm sure we don't have any student by the name of Carson Wells."

"Are you sure?" I asked. "He said that he was part of the Atlanta Fulton County High group."

The man said, "I'm the lead chaperone and we brought a small group. I can assure you we don't have a Carson Wells."

Now that was strange. Maybe I had gotten his school mixed up. Or maybe even his name. Maybe it was Larson or something like that. No, I wasn't crazy. He'd said his name was Carson.

"Sheridan, do you have that picture you took of us at the beach yesterday?"

Sheridan fumbled in her purse, which was strapped around her body. "Yeah." She took her phone out and began thumbing through her pictures.

"Here," she said, handing me the picture that Carson and I had taken last night.

"Yeah, right here," I said, showing the picture to the man. "That's Carson. He's a student at Fulton County High."

The man leaned in and peered at the screen. "Mmm, nope."

"What do you mean, nope?"

"Just what I said. That's not one of our kids." He actually seemed relieved.

I stood with my mouth gaped open. "Are you freaking kidding me?"

"Nope. I know all our kids and that's not one of them."

"Then who is this?" I said.

He shrugged like he couldn't be of any assistance to me.

I turned to Sheridan, who was standing there, just as shocked. "They don't have a Carson. And now, I'm starting to think maybe Carson Wells doesn't even exist."

Carson wasn't who he'd said he was. Evian was missing. If I wasn't worried before, I definitely was now. And I had no idea what kind of game Carson was running, but my gut told me it wasn't good. And now, I not only wanted to find Evian, I felt like I *had to* find her!

Chapter 10

I took a deep breath, dialed three numbers, then quickly hung up the phone. It was taking everything in my power to make this phone call. I knew that I needed to stop putting it off, but more than anything I was wondering why in the world I was scared of Tamara Collins. Yes, she was my boss, but I was the star of *Rumor Central*. So why was I scared to call and tell her this?

I'd wanted to go straight to Shay's room and tell her about Carson, but Tamara had been blowing up my phone and I needed to check in with her first.

Just dial the number, I told myself as I punched in the number to Tamara's cell. When I'd added international calling to my cell phone, I'd had no idea that I would be using it for this.

"Hey, lady—what's going on," Tamara said, answering on the second ring.

"Yeah, nothing much," I said, trying to keep my voice steady. "I'm just in Cancun."

She laughed. "Umm, yeah, I know. I'm sure you're having a blast, but I also hope you've got some good stories." Tamara knew I had been uneasy about bringing the camera along, but I also knew how this game was played. At the end of the day, that's all that she was really worried about. I decided to stop trying to put it off and just come clean.

"No major dirt yet, but ah, it looks like we may have a little dilemma here," I began.

She stopped laughing and I could only imagine her sitting straight up in her high-back leather chair. "What kind of dilemma?" she asked.

"Well, Evian is missing." I rushed the words out.

"Evian? Former *Miami Diva,* Evian?"

"Yep."

"What do you mean she's missing?"

I sighed. This is not what I was supposed to be doing. I was supposed to playing in the ocean with my friends. "We were playing a little game of truth or dare and um, she kind of was dared to go pick up a strange guy."

Tamara hesitated, then said, "Okay. Hate to hear that, but what does that have to do with us because I'm assuming it does since you said *we* have a problem?"

"Well, I had Marcus, our undercover photographer, follow her, but he said she was boring, so he dumped out for the night and we haven't seen her since."

"What? Maybe she clicked with the guy and they just went off together."

"Well, that's what I initially thought," I replied. "But when she didn't check in and nobody has seen or heard from her, everybody started getting worried."

"Wow, that is scary. I hope you guys find her, but I'm not understanding how this is your problem."

"I'm not understanding either." I let out a long sigh. "It really isn't my problem if you ask me. But some people think that I may be to blame and *Rumor Central* may be liable because I'm the one that dared her."

Tamara was quiet at that admission. "Please tell me that's not true."

"You're the one that wanted some good footage so I dared her and had Marcus follow her. No drama was popping off so I was hoping to get some good dirt or gossip or maybe even some video of her making out." Even saying it now, the idea sounded stupid, like anyone even cared who Evian Javid was getting with.

"Oh my God," Tamara said.

"We're looking for her," I said, trying to ease Tamara's concerns. I even lied and told Tamara the police were involved. I hadn't dared call the police for real because naturally, the first call they would make would be to Evian's people. "So don't worry about it. We've got it handled. I just wanted to keep you updated."

"What if this is another Natalee Holloway case?" she said, her voice filled with concern.

"Why does everybody keep talking about Natalee Holloway?"

"That case got worldwide attention." I could hear her up and pacing. "Where's Marcus now?"

"I don't know," I said.

"You need to get with him. You said you guys were looking for Evian?"

"Yes," I said.

"Okay, call Quincy, too. He needs to follow you everywhere you go. Not only for liability reasons, but who knows what you will turn up? If you get something good, it could bring in some awesome numbers."

I was a little shocked, although I don't know why. "So, you're concerned about ratings?" I asked.

"I'm always concerned about ratings," she replied matter-of-factly.

"Do you know what kind of powerhouse story we'd have if we broke up an American kidnapping ring in Cancun? Oh, I can see the headlines now."

Tamara was going off on a tangent, and I could tell there was nothing I could say to change her mind.

But still I had to try. "Tamara, this is serious. I don't think we need to be trying to think about ratings."

"Sweetheart, don't be mistaken. We always think about ratings," Tamara said. "Now find Quincy. I'll get in touch with him as well and I want him rolling on every single thing you do."

"All right, talk to you later. Check back in soon." She hung up the phone before I could say another word. In fact, I sat there staring at my phone.

No, she didn't just hang up in my face. Not only was I caught up in the middle of some drama in Evian's disappearance, but now I was expected to film the whole thing for ratings? As much as I loved my job, sometimes things like this made me hate it.

Chapter 11

I knew one thing; I was tired as all get out. This was not my idea of fun in the sun and right about now, I wished that I had never met Evian Javid. The last thing I wanted to do was spend my time racing around this island trying to find her. Shay had seemed just as shocked when I'd told her Carson was a phony and that had only made us all worry more. So, we'd spent the last three hours combing every hotel looking for her, Carson, or any information.

"I think we've done all we can do," I finally told Shay. The sun was setting and we had literally lost a whole day behind this mess. "Let's just head back to the hotel."

Shay looked defeated but didn't fight me, thank goodness.

"I'm especially worried because we were supposed to take our spring break senior picture at the breakfast this morning and she didn't show up. Evian wouldn't miss that picture," Shay said as she, Sheridan, and I made our way back to our hotel. Quincy was lurking in the background. He really was good at his job because I'd almost forgotten that he'd been trailing us. Suddenly, I remembered that I'd missed the picture, too, which only made me more aggravated.

But on top of my anger, I was actually getting a little nervous now, too, but what could we do?

"I'm going to go back to my room," Shay said. "Maybe Evian left a message or something."

I didn't know what to say so I just followed her inside. I was going to go to my room and change. I felt all sticky and nasty now that I had been traipsing all over looking for Evian.

We had just stepped on the elevator when Shay's phone beeped, signaling an incoming text. "Maybe that's Evian," she said, scrambling to get the purse out of her back pocket.

Her mouth dropped open in horror as she read.

"What? What does it say?" Sheridan asked.

" 'We have your girl,' " Shay read. " 'We will call in one hour for further instructions. No cops.' "

"OMG," Sheridan said. "Is that a ransom text?"

"That's what it looks like," Shay replied. She was shaking like she was terrified. "Evian must've given them my number."

I shook my head. I couldn't believe this.

"Oh my God." Shay fell back against the wall of the elevator. "So somebody *does* have her."

"Maybe somebody's just playing a joke." That's the only thing I could think to say.

Shay shook the phone at me. "Does this look like a joke to you?" she said.

"Okay," Sheridan added. "I'm getting a little nervous myself."

I know I probably should've been the one trying to calm them down, but I needed someone to calm *me* down.

"So, what are we going to do?" Sheridan asked. I still couldn't figure out how this had become a *we* project.

"We're all going to go to my room and wait on that phone call," Shay said. "The good news is if she gave them my number, that means she's still alive."

"See, all this talk about ransom and dead or alive is way above my pay grade," I said, repeating something I'd heard someone on TV once say. "We need to call the police."

"No!" Shay said, pointing the phone at me. "You see they said no cops."

"Can't you just call us and tell us what they say?" I replied. I didn't scare easy, but this was definitely making me uneasy.

"No, we're all in this together," Shay snapped.

I really wanted to remind her that Evian wasn't my friend anymore. That was her girl. Therefore, this was *her* problem.

But if I was being truthful, I knew that the only reason she had taken the dare was because of me, and the last thing I wanted was to have to explain to her family what role I'd played in her disappearance. No, we just needed to find her.

"Fine," I said, motioning for Shay to get off the elevator when the doors opened on her floor. "We'll go to your room and wait on the call."

Sheridan looked like she wanted to protest, but she followed anyway. Inside, Shay's room was eerily quiet as we waited for the phone to ring.

After about fifty minutes, Shay stood. "We got ten minutes. I'm gonna use the restroom real quick."

None of us said a word as she dashed off. I just wanted this all to be over.

Not two minutes after the bathroom door closed, her cell phone rang.

"Shay!" I yelled.

"I'm coming! Answer it!" I heard the toilet flush.

I pressed the button for the speaker phone.

"Hello," I said.

"Are these the rich girl's friends?" the voice said.

"Yes," I replied, willing Shay to hurry up and get her butt out here. I felt a sigh of relief as the door opened and Shay came running out.

"I'm gonna need five hundred thousand dollars if you wanna see your girl alive again," the raspy voice said.

Five hundred thousand dollars? Was he crazy? I didn't need to see Evian alive again.

"Here, it's for you," I told Shay as I handed her the phone. She looked confused as she held the phone.

"Yeah," Shay began.

"Did you hear what I said?" the man repeated.

"Yeah, but um, where are we supposed to get that kind of money from?"

Sheridan stood and watched in shock. Me, I was easing toward the door.

"Find a way," the man said. "Or find your friend's body. I'll be in touch in twenty-four hours."

The line went dead with Shay standing there, holding the phone. Finally, she looked at me and Sheridan and said, "We have to come up with five hundred thousand dollars."

"*We* don't have to do anything," I said.

"You know what? I'm tired of doing this with you," Shay said. She picked up the hotel phone, pressed zero, and then said, "Yes, I'd like to place a collect call to Miami, Florida."

"Who are you calling?" I asked.

"I'm calling Evian's brother," Shay said. "What's his name? Clinton? I'm sure him and his mafia friends can get over here and help us."

Sheridan raced over to the phone, then put her hand on the button to hang the phone up. "But I thought you said they were going to blame us," she said, panicked.

"They're not going to blame *us*," Shay replied, motioning between her and Sheridan. "They're going to blame *her*." She pointed at me. "She's the one that dared Evian to go with that guy. She's the one that introduced everyone to Carson."

"Fine," I huffed. This was wrong on so many levels. But I knew that Shay was right. "So, we're just supposed to give these people five hundred thousand dollars? Where are we supposed to get five hundred thousand dollars from?"

"I don't know," Shay replied. "Call your dad."

"You call *your* dad," I said. Shay might not have been as rich as me, but they were still loaded. Her father probably wore five hundred thousand dollars' worth of jewelry around his neck.

"Between us, we're going to have to come up with the money," Shay said.

"Let's not and say we did," I replied. "Let's just call the cops and when it's time to give them the money, the police can bust the crooks, we get Evian back, and we take our happy behinds home."

"Yeah, if only it was that easy," Shay replied.

"All I know is that I didn't sign up for all of this," I snapped.

"And you think I did?" Shay said. "You think Evian did?"

I exchanged glances with Sheridan before saying, "Okay, fine. Let me go back to my room and make some calls and see how much I can come up with. You do the same and maybe between all of us, we can get enough money."

Shay nodded, seemingly relieved. "Cool. I'll catch back up with you guys in a couple of hours."

Sheridan quietly followed me out. Once we were on the elevator, she turned to me and said, "Maya, I want to help and I might be able to get my hands on a few thousand, but I can't just come up off that kind of money. My mom would have a million and one questions, then it would just be added drama."

"Girl, please. It would be the same with my dad," I said, pushing the button to the penthouse floor. "And besides, I don't know Evian like that just to be giving up that kind of money."

"But I thought you told Shay you were going to work on coming up with the money," Sheridan said.

"I just told her that so we could get out of there. Even if I had five hundred thousand in my purse right now, I wouldn't be giving it to some kidnappers for a girl I don't even cut for."

We stepped off the elevator. "I'm sorry. I hope Shay works it all out," I said. "But I'm done."

Sheridan didn't protest as she followed me into our suite.

Chapter 12

After the stressful day I'd had yesterday, I was going to chill today. Shay had called last night and when we'd ignored her calls, she'd come to our suite, banging on the door like a lunatic. Finally, she'd left, but she was back this morning, acting such a fool that I knew it was just a matter of time before hotel security came.

"What?" I said, finally swinging open the door to the suite.

She barged in, past me. "I don't know what kind of games you're playing, Maya Morgan, but I'm not the one!"

I let out a heavy sigh. "Shay, I'm not playing any games. I was exhausted yesterday and came back here and we all fell asleep."

She folded her arms and glared at me. "And nobody heard me banging on the door last night."

I shook my head and shrugged. "Nope, sorry."

"Whatever, Maya. How much money were you able to get your hands on?" she asked. "These people aren't playing. They called again this morning."

I walked over to the refrigerator and got one of the orange juices out of the minibar.

"I'm sorry," I said, opening my juice. "But I just can't get my hands on that kind of money. The cash advance on my credit cards only go up to five thousand and I tried, but it won't even let me withdraw that here," I lied. I took a swig of my juice. "You know, they gotta protect their clients from fraud and stuff."

Sheridan and Kennedi emerged from their rooms. Shay looked around and at all of us.

"I guess you all think this is some kind of game." No one said anything. "Fine, I guess we just need to call her people and get the money from them," Shay threatened.

"You know, I think that's what we should do," I said, walking over to get my cell phone off the coffee table.

"What are you doing?" Sheridan asked as I picked up the phone and started dialing.

"I'm about to tell Evian's family."

"What?" Sheridan said. "Have you lost your mind?"

"No. This is their problem, not ours. They need to be flying here today with a suitcase full of money."

Shay jumped up. "No!"

"Whatever," I mumbled, ignoring her. I was tired of this whole thing. I tried to recall the name of her brother's restaurant. "Yes, I need the number to Javid's Middle Eastern Cuisine," I said when the 411 operator came on.

Sheridan's mouth was open. She finally said, "Um, you *do* know who her family is?"

"You *do* know I don't care," I said while I waited on the number. Of course I knew all about her family, but at this point, we needed to do *something*.

"Who is her family?" Kennedi asked.

"Rumor has it that they are in the mafia," Sheridan said.

"It ain't a rumor," Shay said.

"Mafia?" Kennedi replied.

"Yes. I heard her brother Lyn tried to get this meat packer in downtown Miami to pay some money he owed and the guy tried to stiff him. Workers came in the next day and this guy was hanging from his hands and his feet, tied up along with all of the other meat in the freezer. They had skinned him alive and let him bleed to death right there in the freezer," Sheridan said. She looked like she was telling a horror story.

"What?" Kennedi said. "Are you serious?"

"That's just a rumor. We don't even know if that's true," I said, just as the operator came on to give me the number. I pushed the button to be automatically connected. It was after nine so hopefully, someone would be at the office.

"That's just one of *many* rumors," Sheridan said.

"And do you really want to find out if it's true?" Shay said.

"Whatever," I said. "Evian's people need to be down here looking for her. This has nothing to do with me."

My heart actually started racing when I heard someone say, "Hello, Middle Eastern Cuisine Corporate Office."

"Yes. I need to speak with Clinton Javid, the owner. This is a friend of his sister, Evian. It's pretty important," I said.

"Yes, this is Mr. Javid's assistant, Delana," the woman who answered said. "How may I help you?"

"Well I'm trying to get in touch with Mr. Javid," I replied. "It's in regards to Evian."

The woman paused. "Evian's not available."

"I know that. I'm not looking for Evian," I told the woman. "I'm actually here with her."

"Mr. Javid is in a meeting."

"Well, this is important. Evian is kind of ummm . . . she's kind of. . . ."

"What?" the woman said, panicked. Her voice suddenly lost all professionalism. "Oh my God. Please tell me nothing happened to Evian. That is Mr. Javid's heart. He loves that girl to death."

"No, no, Evian's fine."

She actually released a sigh of relief.

"I know they're close," I found myself saying. Something was telling me to feel this situation out before I started running my mouth.

"That's an understatement," Delana said. "Just ask her ex-boyfriend." The woman lowered her voice. "He pushed her and let's just say he doesn't have a hand anymore."

"A hand?" I said, stunned.

"People are going to learn that this family is not one you want to mess with," Delana said. Then, as if catching herself, she said, "I'm sorry. Let me see if I can get Mr. Javid."

I actually started trembling, and I didn't even scare easily. "Um, no. No need. Evian just wanted to let him know that she was having a great time and that she would be home this weekend," I hurriedly said.

The woman was momentarily quiet. "Oh, okay."

"Something's wrong with her cell phone, so she just wanted to call the restaurant and check in . . . What, Evian?" I said. I don't know what made me try to pretend I was talking to Evian, but I felt that I needed to clean up this mess. "Do you want me to get him? Oh, okay. I'll let him know." Sheridan, Kennedi, and Shay were looking at me like I was crazy. I ignored them and kept talking. "Evian said that's fine, she'll just catch up with Clinton later."

"Okay, well, tell her I said hello," Delana said. "And enjoy herself."

"Will do." I quickly hung the phone up.

"What? What just happened?" Sheridan said.

I let out a big sigh. "Okay, so you guys were right," I admitted. "I'm not about to tell Evian's family that she's missing." I turned to everyone. "I guess we just have to come up with the money or find her."

Kennedi leaned back and kicked her legs up on the coffee table. "*We* don't have to do anything. Good luck."

"So you're really going to leave us to do this by ourselves?" I asked.

"Yep," Kennedi said.

I didn't have time to argue. Getting the money wasn't an option, so the only other option was back to searching, which officially made this the worst trip ever.

Chapter 13

This was getting us nowhere. And right about now, not only was I sick and tired of Evian, I was sick and tired of racing around this place looking for her. Like what were we really going to do if we found her? Beat up the kidnappers and take her back? I'd called Travis and he was trying to get me some money, but the most I would be willing to come up off of was twenty thousand and I didn't even want to do that. Plus, I didn't know what good twenty thousand would do anyway.

"Back so soon?" Kennedi said, laughing as she popped a strawberry in her mouth. "Thank you, hun," she said to the bare-chested hunk who was apparently just wrapping up her massage. "Hector, you have some magical hands. Bill it to the room."

I looked at all the muscles in Hector's body. "Can I get a massage, too?"

He laughed, but I didn't see anything funny. "Sorry, I have another appointment to get to," he said.

"Thank you," Kennedi said, holding the door open.

"Wow," I said. "So we're out traipsing all over this island and you're up here getting a massage. Like really?"

"Yes, really. I keep trying to tell y'all. That's your girl and not mine. But the good news is, Hector had some gossip I think you'll be interested in."

"What?" I asked, grateful for at least that. That way I could get Tamara off my back.

"Before Hector came to me, he had an appointment with Darian Mathis." Kennedi got comfortable on the sofa. This must've been juicy because she was grinning like she had a big secret.

"Darian, the pop star?"

"Yep. And guess who she was in her room with?"

"Who?" I asked.

"She was in the room with Jay Blackmon."

"The rapper?"

"Yes, ma'am." Kennedi turned up her lips.

"Wait a minute, but isn't he married to . . . ?"

"Yes, he is," she said, cutting me off. "Olivia Martinez's husband of two months is chilling in the suite down the hall with another woman."

Oh, wow. Everyone had talked about Olivia and Jay getting married. They were both superstars in their own right, but they were only nineteen.

"Wow," I said. "Let me call Quincy and tell him to stake out their room." I paused. "Dang, how am I going to find out what room it is?"

"You need to hire me," Kennedi said, whipping out a piece of paper and holding it toward me. "They're in suite 403."

I high-fived her, then grabbed the phone and called Quincy. This would definitely make Tamara and Dexter happy. I needed something because so far I hadn't come up with anything for *Rumor Central: On the Road.*

I had just fired off the information for Quincy to come meet me when someone came banging at my door. I wasn't in the mood for a party right now. I needed to take a nap and regroup, so I hoped this wasn't any of my friends trying to get the party started.

"Who is it?" I yelled.

"It's me, Shay."

I rolled my eyes as I opened the door. "What's up?"

She burst through the door. "I think I know where Evian is. Let's go!"

"How do you know where Evian is?" I asked.

"Because I called one of my dad's friends and had them do a trace on Evian's phone. She has a GPS on it, so they were able to locate her."

I was stunned Shay hadn't even said anything about having Evian's phone traced.

"Why didn't they do that in the first place while you had me running around like crazy trying to find her?"

"Look, we've been working on it. It's not as easy as it sounds. Just come on."

"Ugh," I groaned, walking back into the suite to get my shoes. Sheridan had just come out of her bedroom, where she'd been taking a nap. "Come on, Sheridan."

"Unh-unh," Sheridan said. She plopped down on the sofa next to Kennedi. "You got this. I'm exhausted."

I looked over at Kennedi, who rolled her eyes. "You know better than to ask me. Be careful out there."

"This sucks. Big time," I groaned as I followed Shay out.

We had just reached the end of the hallway when we bumped into Quincy.

He caught me, keeping me from losing my balance.

"Hey, where's the fire? Are you leaving?" he asked. "I was coming to meet you."

Suddenly, I had an idea. If we were going to find Evian, Tamara was right, we needed it all caught on tape. "Quincy, you know what, where's your gear?"

"It's in my car. I'm parked out front. Why?"

I turned to Shay. "Okay, let's go, Quincy can drive us."

"Drive you where?" he asked, confused.

"I'll tell you all about it in the car," I said. "Right now, we need to go save someone." I lowered my voice and added, "And hopefully, get us a banging story in the process."

Chapter 14

I felt like I was seriously in the middle of some double-oh-seven mess.

"How do you know she's in there?" I whispered to Shay.

"I don't," she replied. "All I know is this is where the call was traced to."

We were in some rundown neighborhood, at what looked like a crumbling duplex. There were burglar bars on the windows, and the place looked like it should've been condemned several years ago. This was definitely the part of Cancun they kept out of the brochures.

"*Hola! ¿En qué puedo ayudarle?*"

I hadn't even noticed the little boy playing on the side of the house. He looked like he couldn't be more than eight or nine. He was dirty, and wore raggedy clothes.

Shay and I exchanged glances. I'd taken a few years of Spanish but since I hadn't really been paying attention, I only knew a few words.

"*¿Hablas inglés?*" I asked.

The little boy stood there for a minute, then said in choppy English, "What you want? Herb?" He stared at us like he was really ready to conduct a drug transaction.

"Umm, yeah," Shay said.

"A'ight, Pedro is inside," the little boy said, motioning toward the front door.

Shay motioned for me to follow her up the walkway. I couldn't believe she was acting like she was going to conduct a drug transaction. What if he was a miniature undercover cop? I couldn't do a Mexican prison!

"Why don't we just ask that little boy if Evian is in there?" I whispered as I followed her.

"For him to go warn the kidnapper? No," Shay said.

"Are you sure the GPS traced to the exact address?" I asked. "I thought a GPS system could only do a vicinity."

I was nervous as all get-out. Shay may have been hood, but neither of us was cut out for this.

"Yeah," she said, still whispering.

I shook my head. Something about this didn't feel right. "Well, why don't we just call the police then?" I said again.

"They said no cops. Besides, we don't have time to wait on the police. We barely had time to wait on your stupid cameraman," she said, pointing to Quincy, who was across the street, rolling the entire time.

"You said you were okay with filming."

"Well, I didn't mean leave my friend in danger while you set everything up."

She was talking about how Quincy had made us stop around the corner while he got his camera gear set up. I knew if we rescued Evian—if she *was* even here—and I didn't catch it on film, that could be my job. So, it wasn't going to kill her to wait an extra three minutes.

Personally, I thought this was all going to be a bust anyway, but I made the motion to Quincy to make sure he was rolling. He had his long-distance lens on, so he gave me the thumbs-up to let me know he was good to go.

Shay knocked on the door to the duplex. My heart was racing. This was the dumbest idea ever. How were we—two teenaged girls—going to just knock on some drug-dealing kidnapper's door and say, "Hey, give us our friend back"? Realizing that we hadn't thought this plan all the way through, I was just about to make a U-turn and beeline out of there, when the door swung open.

"Ay, mamacita," the man who answered the door said. "What can I do for you?" Like the little boy, his English was choppy and hard to understand.

"Nothing," Shay replied. She'd told me to just play along and that's exactly what I was doing. "We just came to see if we could get a little of the good stuff."

The guy broke out into a big smile. "Ah, American girls looking for that herb," he said.

"Yeah, that's it," I said, trying to play along. "We need some good herb."

He looked me up and down, then did the same with Shay before saying, "All right, wait right here."

"Now what?" I whispered as soon as he took off inside the house.

"I just needed to make sure someone lives here."

"Okay, so now we know. Again, let's call the cops," I said, tugging at her arm.

"How about I distract the guy and you go in there after her?" Shay said.

"How about, you have lost your freakin' mind. I don't know who's in there, what kind of weapon they have, and oh yeah, today's my day off from my superhero duties!"

"Look." Shay turned to face me. "We don't have much choice. Evian is in there. I know it," she whispered. "I feel it in my gut, and we need to do what we can to get her out."

The guy opened the door back up. "Here's that herb. It's some real good stuff," he said, shaking a small baggie in front of us.

"Mmm, yeah that's what I'm talking about," Shay said.

She looked over her shoulder at me to give me the cue. Then all of a sudden she fell to the ground, shaking.

"Oh no," I said, hurrying to her side. "She's having a seizure!"

"What? What you mean she's having a seizure?" the guy said. "What am I supposed to do about that?" he yelled.

"I don't know! Here, grab her! Grab her!" I said as Shay shook violently on the ground. I had to give it to her—she looked like she was straight in the middle of an epileptic seizure. It was extremely convincing. The boy was freaking out.

"Help me get her inside," I said.

"I'm not taking her in there!" he said, panicked.

"Do you want her to die right here?"

"I don't care. I don't know her!"

"Yeah, but she also has this." I pointed to a button on her necklace. "This is her seizure alarm. Anytime it goes off, the cops come. Is that what you want?"

I was grateful that he didn't realize that was actually a Tiffany charm necklace.

"What cops?" he said. *"Salir ahora!"*

"Huh?" I said.

"Go! Leave! Now!" he repeated.

"How do you expect me to get her out of here?" I said.

This idea had seemed dumb at first, but it actually looked like it was working. Especially when the guy took a deep breath and said, "Fine," and then opened the door. He muttered what I'm sure were curse words in Spanish.

"Can you help me get her inside?" I asked, trying to lift Shay up.

"Naw, *mami*. I can't do none of that," he said.

"Fine!" I barked as I tried to get Shay up. She continued shaking. "Would you chill out?" I whispered.

She calmed down enough for me to lift and get her inside.

"I need a wet towel," I said to him once I'd gotten her inside and on the dusty old sofa.

"Look, no hospital," he said.

"Can you just get me a wet towel?"

He reluctantly ran and got a wet towel.

"Is there someone else here who can help?" I said.

"No, just me." He looked around. "*¡Ándale!*"

Shay and I exchanged glances and that was our cue. As soon as he leaned over the sink and started wringing out a towel, we both pounced on him as he struggled to get loose. Shay broke free, grabbed a pot, and coldcocked him upside the head. Once he was down, I took off running and began looking room to room. When I opened the second door, I wanted to cry when I saw Evian tied to a post inside. She was dirty, her eyes were puffy, and her hair was matted, which for Evian, Ms. Clairol herself, was major.

"Evian!" I said, racing toward her. "Are you okay?" I snatched off the tape that was covering her mouth.

"Does it look like I'm okay?" she snapped.

I gave her a pass because being held hostage was enough to make anybody crazy.

"I've been held hostage for three days. It's been a nightmare," she said, struggling to free her hands.

I quickly untied her hands. "Come on, let's get out of here."

"Where's Pedro?" she said.

"We knocked him out," Shay said, appearing next to me. "Let's get out of here before he comes to."

Evian quickly unraveled the rope around her legs and untied herself.

We managed to get out just as we saw Pedro stirring again. "Mmm," he moaned.

"Let's go," Shay said. When we raced outside, Quincy was right on the front lawn, filming.

"Is she okay?" he asked. He didn't stop filming though as we dragged Evian out. The minute we got her outside, Evian began sobbing even more.

"Come on, it's going to be okay," I said.

I knew she had to be scared out of her mind, but it seemed like when she saw the camera, she amped up her tears.

I shook off that thought. Now wasn't the time for cattiness. Evian had been through it. Then, suddenly, it dawned on me that I was the one who had saved her. I motioned toward Quincy.

"Make sure you keep that camera on me," I whispered as I limped past him. Yes, we'd just rescued Evian, maybe even saved her life, but no one should ever get it twisted. Maya Morgan was the real star of this show.

Chapter 15

I knew Evian had been through the wringer, but this chick was taking it to a whole different level. We had just pulled into our hotel and had barely gotten Evian out of the car when she spotted our chaperone.

"Miss Martin," Evian cried, running into her arms.

"Evian! Where have you been?" Our lead chaperone hugged her tightly, relief blanketing her face. Shay had finally broken down last night and told her that Evian had been missing. Needless to say, she was an absolute wreck.

Evian collapsed in Miss Martin's arms and she guided her down onto the sofa.

"I was kidnapped—it was so horrible. I thought I was going to die," she sobbed.

I couldn't do anything but roll my eyes. She was so extra. Several people began gathering around us.

"Oh my God, are you okay? Someone call the police!" Miss Martin shouted.

"No, no. I'm just glad to be out of there," Evian said.

She'd laid with her head in Shay's lap the whole ride back to the hotel. I had sat up front with Quincy so I hadn't seen her crying, but I had definitely been able to hear that she hadn't been as overboard as she was right now.

Quincy was still filming. He was a true cameraman. Nothing got in the way of him getting his video.

"You can stop filming now," I told him.

"Naw, Tamara told me to make sure I got everything," he replied.

"We got enough," I repeated.

"Look, I'm just doing my job," he said, moving out of the way so he could continue filming. He was actually working my nerves, too.

Hotel security came racing over, and Evian's tears went up a notch.

"Okay, ma'am, please tell us what happened," one of the security officers said.

Evian took a deep breath, like she was trying to calm herself down.

"The other day, I was at the bar," she began. "I don't know what happened, but the next thing I knew, I was being grabbed."

I raised an eyebrow. *Grabbed?* We'd asked everyone about her and no one had mentioned anything about seeing her being grabbed.

"Ma'am, I need to get more details," the security officer said. "What did the person that grabbed you look like? Exactly where in the hotel were you? Did anyone see you?"

Suddenly, Evian let out a loud sob. "I can't! I just can't talk about this anymore. I just want to go home. I thought I was going to die!"

"Not now," Miss Martin told the security officer as she pushed him back.

"Police are on the way," another security officer said.

"I don't want to press charges," Evian cried. "I just want to go home."

"Oh, my God," Shay said, hugging Evian. "Can't you see she's been through enough?"

"Ma'am, it's just a few questions," the security officer said.

Evian clutched Miss Martin tightly. "Please, Miss Martin. I promise if you just let me go home, my daddy won't sue you or the school."

At the mention of suing, Miss Martin tensed up. She knew that she probably would be in big trouble if this got out. She'd be smart to keep Evian calm. "Okay, that's it," Miss Martin said firmly. "We're done. This poor thing has been through the wringer. She's safe now, and I just want her to rest until we leave in the morning. I will get her settled, then I'll come give a report."

Oh, Evian was good. I'd seen firsthand what she'd endured, so it wasn't that I didn't believe her. I just couldn't believe how she was taking this to a whole other level. And I had the strangest feeling that this was only the beginning.

Chapter 16

"What's up, cuz?" Travis said as I walked in the house. Instead of helping me with my bags though, he plopped down on the sofa. "Tell me everything I missed." He crossed his legs and put them up on my mom's Italian marble table.

"You're about to be missing those feet if you don't get them off my mom's coffee table," I told him.

He laughed. "Since you've been gone, I've gotten auntie and uncle wrapped around my finger."

"I thought you were going home?" I asked.

The look on his face turned sad. "I did. But mama wanted me to come back early because she's in the hospital and said she didn't want me to spend all my days cooped up with her."

"Hospital? Is she okay?"

Travis nodded. "Yeah, she's fine now. She's getting her treatment thanks to your dad, and hopefully, she'll be back to normal in no time."

"That's good," I said, dropping my purse onto the counter. "But I'm going to lie down. I need to decompress after the horrible week I had."

He actually sat up. "Horrible? What are you talking about? What happened?"

"I don't even know where to begin." I sighed.

"What? So Cancun wasn't the bomb? That's all you were talking about was how much fun you were going to have."

"Yeah, that was before Evian got kidnapped."

"Your girl Evian?"

"She's not my girl," I said, rolling my eyes. "As a matter of fact, she's not anything to me but a pain in the behind."

"Back up. What do you mean, she was kidnapped?"

I needed to get my story together. How I was going to tell everyone what happened to Evian without revealing my part in it with the truth-or-dare game?

"She went off with this dude and she never came back," I said.

"What?" he repeated, sounding like a broken record.

"Yeah. Messed up, I know," I replied. "She went for a walk with this guy. Then just up and went missing. Long story short, Shay tracked her down, we went in and saved her, and now, she's acting like she's in some action movie, like she's a damsel in distress."

Travis shook his head in disbelief. "Wow. So I did miss out on some fun?"

"Trust, there was nothing fun about this whole experience. In fact, we couldn't even enjoy ourselves because everyone was freaking out over Evian."

Travis didn't know Evian well. By the time he had moved here, *Miami Divas* had already been canceled, so he really only knew her from around school.

"Wow. I heard that her peeps were connected to the mob or something. You think that's why she was kidnapped?"

I shrugged. Truth be told, I was tired of thinking about Evian, period. "I don't know how the kidnapper would've had any way of knowing that. But I can tell you none of us wanted to be the one to have to come back and tell her family that their little princess was missing, so I'm just glad we found her."

"We?"

"Yep. Me and Shay. All by ourselves."

"Where were the police?" Travis was engrossed like he was watching a good movie.

"We didn't even call the cops. We found out where she was, went in, and saved her ourselves."

"Something isn't adding up," Travis said, skeptically. "What kind of bootleg kidnappers were these?"

I shrugged. "I have no idea. I just know I'm glad it's over."

"Wow," he said again.

"Can you say something else?" I don't know why every little thing was irritating me, but it was. I'd been irritated on the whole plane ride home, then when we'd landed and Tamara had started blowing up my phone (I'd yet to call her back). Maybe I was just mad that not only had the Spring Break Fling been a bust, but other than Evian and Jay Blackmon, I didn't have any real dirt I could use on *Rumor Central*.

"It's just a trip," Travis said.

"Naw, what's a trip is how she has everyone feeling all sorry for her. She's being such a drama queen behind all of this."

He laughed like something was really funny. "Can you let that girl have her moment?"

"I'm the one that saved her anyway."

That made him sit up. "So, tell me about that. How did you save her?"

I finally smiled. "Tune into the show next week because it was all caught on tape."

Travis laughed. "Of course it was. You weren't about to go in with your superhero cape on and *not* be rolling. Because Evian isn't the only one that likes to shine."

"Whatever, Travis. I'm tired. Can you get my bags?" I stood and pointed toward the door. "They're in my trunk."

"Un-unh." He reached up and grabbed the remote, then turned the TV back on. "Do I look like Sui?" he said, referring to our maid, as he put his feet back up on the table and got comfortable.

"Ugh, you make me sick. Where's my mom?"

"Mama!" he yelled. "Maya's back!"

My hands went to my hips. "Excuse me?"

He smiled. "She told me to call her mama."

"Ah, she's not your mother. Aunt Bev is your mother," I said with an attitude.

"Dang, girl, chill out." Travis laughed, then stopped when he saw that I wasn't laughing. "Evian got under your skin for real." I just rolled my eyes.

"Aunt Liza, Maya's back!" he screamed.

"And stop yelling," I snapped. "My mother hates when you yell in the house."

"Hey, sweetheart," my mom said, walking into the living room. She looked her usual fabulous self in a long Diane Von Furstenberg wrap dress.

I paused, waiting for her to go off on Travis, for yelling and for his feet being plopped up on her table.

"When did you get back?" She walked over and gave me a hug.

I just stood there. "Uh, don't you see his feet on your table and him yelling like a caveman?" I said, pointing at my cousin.

My mother squeezed my cheek. "Oh, lighten up, Maya. It's all good, for sheezy." She turned to Travis and giggled.

My mouth dropped open in horror. "Mother, no. Don't ever, ever, ever, *ever* say that again."

"Travis has been teaching me all the latest hip phrases," my mom replied.

"Why would he be doing that?" I asked.

"Chill, cuz," Travis told me. "Me and Mama, I mean Auntie Liza, we've just been hanging, bonding."

"And guess what?" my mom excitedly said. "He also taught me how to Dougie."

"Taught you how to what?"

She raced over to the CD player, pressed a couple of buttons and the "Teach Me How to Dougie" song filled the living room. And then my mother, the prissy, sophisticated Liza Morgan, began doing the Dougie right in the middle of the living room floor. That was astonishing because my mother didn't Dougie, Wobble, Cupid Shuffle, or anything other than waltz. At least she hadn't before I went to Cancun.

"Okay, does someone want to explain where my real mother is?" I yelled over the music as Travis jumped up and joined her.

"Come on, Maya, join us," my mother said, laughing and dancing.

Both of them made me sick and I wasn't in the mood to be playing around. Besides, my mom had never danced with me.

"Where's Daddy?"

"Where is he always? Working," she shouted as that stupid song continued to play.

"Teach me how to Dougie, t-teach me how to Dougie," Travis sang as he danced next to her.

All I could do was stare at both of them. I shook my head as I turned to head up to my room. Now, I knew without a doubt, the whole world had lost its mind.

Chapter 17

"What's up everybody? It's your girl Maya Morgan back from the Spring Break Fling 2014."

I smiled as the camera did a slow pan toward me. I was actually happy to be back on the air. They'd been running teases of Evian's story, and I was about to unveil my dramatic rescue of her. I knew that we'd have a lot of people tuning in because her story had been the talk of the town since we'd gotten back. Not that we didn't already have a lot of viewers. But there had been a lot of interest in the story because Tamara had sent a sneak peek of the video of Evian's rescue to all the major news outlets, not to mention Evian herself had been crying all over national TV.

"Well, our spring break turned into a straight mystery," I said to the camera, "as a former *Miami Diva* and personal friend found herself in the middle of a kidnapping caper. And of course, yours truly happened to be the one to track Evian down. I guess you guys didn't know that I was a super sleuth as well as a super star," I said, flashing a smile at the camera. "But don't take my word for it, see for yourself."

I stood back as the video of our dramatic rescue began playing. Quincy had done a great job of editing it (along with the undercover video) all together to make it look more intense than it actually was.

After the video stopped, every eye in the studio was glued to the screen so I could only imagine the reactions of all the people who were tuned in all over the country. Once the tape was over, my director, Manny, gave me the cue to continue.

"And after the break, we have Evian here and she's going to go live and tell us more about what happened and how she escaped," I said.

I tossed to the break and then waited for the assistant producer to bring Evian on set. Evian had done two other interviews, but she had acted too distraught in those. She was supposed to be coming on *Rumor Central* to tell "the whole story."

Evian was definitely looking fly in her Versace suit and her silver Red Bottoms. I had to give it to her, the girl looked good.

"Hey, Evian," I said.

"Hi, Maya," she replied.

I looked at the big guy who was with her.

"Oh, my family hired security for me," she said nonchalantly. "Everybody is worked up about what happened."

I wondered if she had told her family everything—about the game and me daring her to go off. Since I still had both my arms, I was assuming she hadn't.

"My dad and brothers are super scared of something happening to me, so they wanted to make sure I was protected," Evian continued.

"I can only imagine," Tamara said, coming up beside her. "That had to have been a terrifying experience. But we're so glad that you're all right and here to talk to us."

Evian was grinning like Tamara wasn't the one who had fired her eight months ago.

"Thank you, Tamara. And it's so good to see you."

"Come on, let me get you set up," Manny said, motioning for Evian to come stand next to me. She did and within minutes, we were back on the air.

I knew that I needed to pretend like I was cool with Evian because bitterness was not a good look to have toward your guests. So I said, "I'm here with my girl Evian Javid, who will explain a little bit more about her harrowing ordeal." I turned to face my former costar. "Now, Evian, we know you've been through it. Tell us what happened."

As if on cue, Evian's eyes began to water as she explained how she'd gone up to the bar because she didn't want to play a game of truth or dare (I was grateful that she didn't mention me) and the next thing she knew, someone grabbed her and she'd woken up in a dingy duplex.

"They said they were going to make me into a sex slave," she said, her voice cracking. "I told them that my parents had money and so they were going to do a ransom, but I found out not only were they going to do a ransom, they had no plans to release me. They were going to get the money and *still* keep me as a sex slave. Apparently it's a ring that they're doing in Cancun."

Wow, I thought. She sure had gotten a lot of information for a hostage. And this was the first I'd heard of any sex slave! I mean I know her ordeal had to be frightening, but Evian was definitely milking it for all it was worth. I'm sure her tears were real, but all the stopping to catch her breath and the theatrics of "give me a minute, I can't continue" were just a bit much. Still, I let her continue.

The interview continued for ten more minutes, which in TV time is an eternity. I kept expecting to hear my producer, Dexter, in my ear telling me to wrap it up, but he let us continue. Every time I tried to cut the interview off, Evian kept talking.

Finally I had to say, "Okay, well, we're wishing you all the best." I turned toward the camera. "We are out of time so of course, keep it here on *Rumor Central* because you know I've got the scoop. Until next time, holla at your girl."

The music came up and I removed my earpiece. "Good interview, Evian."

She didn't even respond, just gave me a half smile as Tamara and Dexter came rushing on to the set.

"Oh my God, Evian! That was awesome. You are really a hit with people. Everyone is mesmerized by our story. There are people outside the studio!"

"What kind of people?" Evian excitedly said.

"People who want to talk to you. News media, more press, and some supporters. I've never seen anything like it." Dexter beamed.

"For me?" Evian said, her hand was on her chest like she was just so shocked.

"Yes, girl! You're a star!" Dexter said.

Oh, give me a break, I wanted to scream. Evian wasn't a star. She was a kidnapping victim. *I* was a star. Evian was a wannabe who was taking a tragedy and using it to her advantage.

I was going to be glad when the next big story rolled along, so Evian could crawl back under her rock and go back to being the irrelevant princess she had been before all of this happened.

Chapter 18

Yeah, I had an attitude and I wasn't even bothering to try and hide it. All this hype about Evian was working my last nerve.

"Hey, Maya, do you need anything?" my assistant, Yolanda, asked me. Yolanda was my right hand, and after my disastrous previous assistants (another long story), I was grateful to have her.

"Yeah, I need you to make this story with Evian disappear," I snarled as I tossed my scripts on to my desk. Yolanda could make a lot of stuff happen, but I knew she wouldn't be capable of that. Unfortunately.

She laughed as she looked at the TV screen in the corner of my office. "Yeah, I know. She really is milking it for all it's worth."

"Tell me about it," I said as I side-eyed the TV.

Evian was being interviewed by Terrence J on *Entertainment Tonight*, and she was bringing it full force. The dramatics, the tears. You could've sworn that she had been kidnapped by aliens or something. After my interview yesterday, she'd done *The Today Show* and *Good Morning America*.

"Whatever," I said, turning the TV off. "She needs to enjoy her fifteen minutes of fame because it's about to be up."

Yolanda shook her head doubtfully. "No, it looks like she's parlayed that fifteen minutes into something major." Yolanda caught herself and her smile faded when she saw the way I was looking at her.

"Um, well, if you don't need anything else I'm going to be going," she stammered, before scurrying out of my office.

"Yeah, you do that," I snapped. I didn't mean to be going off on her, but I was in a foul mood since yesterday. Dexter and Tamara hadn't stopped raving about how Evian seemed to have morphed into a whole different person since the *Miami Divas*. And Evian was eating the praise up.

I pushed aside thoughts of Evian and was going through some of my e-mails when my office phone rang.

"It's Maya," I said, answering.

"Hey, Maya, Ms. Collins would like to see you in her office," Tamara's assistant, Kelley, said.

I groaned. My attitude was so bad I just wanted to go home, but I decided to go see what it was that Tamara wanted. I made my way to her office, where she was sitting at her desk poring over some papers. It always amazed me to see how cluttered her desk was, especially because the rest of her office was so together. Everything in her office was first class. She had an imported marble desk, plush leather chairs, and a bearskin rug. Her walls were covered with awards that she had won for her television shows, and of course, pictures of every celebrity under the sun.

"Hey, Tamara, what's up? Kelley said you wanted to see me."

"Come in. Have a seat."

"What's going on?" I asked as I sat down in the chair in front of her desk.

"Well," Tamara began, looking up from her papers, "we

were going over some of the numbers and yesterday's show gave us some of our highest ratings in weeks."

"That's good to know," I said, still wondering why this information couldn't wait until in the morning.

"But we've also been monitoring something else that seems to be generating quite a few ratings."

I raised my eyebrow as I waited for her to continue. The look on her face told me that she was treading lightly.

"Well, I know this situation with Evian started out tragically, but her round of television and radio interviews has given us some ideas."

That made me sit up, my eyebrows raised, my head cocked. "What kind of ideas?"

"Well, we're exploring a couple of things. One includes"—Tamara took a deep breath like she was trying to psych herself up to finish—"one includes having Evian be a correspondent on *Rumor Central* just because of her notoriety and—"

I cut her off. "I don't think so." I knew Tamara was the boss, but I was the *show*. And it would be a cold day before I let Evian ride her manufactured publicity into my spotlight.

"No, hear me out," Tamara continued. She pulled out several magazines and newspapers and spread them out across her desk. "Between Evian's media coverage, her notoriety, the pizzazz that she seems to have picked up from somewhere—because she sure didn't have that when she was with *Miami Divas*—with all of that, we just think we could market the heck out of this. Like it or not, Evian is bankable right now."

Tamara must've been smoking some potent drugs because she was clearly high.

"So is Maya Morgan," I said. "In fact Maya Morgan is *always* bankable and didn't need to be kidnapped in order to be relevant."

Tamara shook her head as a small smile crept up on her

face. "Somehow I knew you wouldn't be too keen on this idea, but I really wish that you would consider it."

"Wow," I said. "Are you, like, serious?" I wanted to tell her that if she was, I just needed to turn in my notice right now because I would quit before I shared my show with the likes of Evian Javid.

"We haven't worked out all the details," Tamara admitted. "We were just tossing around some ideas, but we need to make a decision soon."

This was some B.S. "I can't believe you guys think because Evian was kidnapped and knows how to turn on the waterworks, that means that she's ready for TV."

Tamara shrugged like she didn't expect me to get it. "Well, again, we're still trying to work out details, but we definitely would like to take this to the next level with Evian. I respect that you don't want her on *Rumor Central,* but I'll figure something out."

All I could do was shake my head. Just wow. I didn't have any serious beef with Evian. I just didn't think she had what it took to "take it to the next level." But judging from the look in Tamara's eyes, all she saw were ratings and for some warped reason, she seemed to think that Evian could bring those ratings to us. I don't know why she couldn't see that even if people did start out watching some stupid show that Evian was on, they wouldn't stick around because she wasn't star material. It would only be a matter of time before they saw that she was one big boring blob. And no kidnapping, sex enslavement, or any other sob story could ever change that.

Chapter 19

I had never been so happy to hear the bell ring. Today had been one of those days.

I had already been in a foul mood when I arrived, but that make-up calculus test had just made things worse. Then, the way Evian was parading around like she was Barbara Walters or something just burned my skin. I needed to get off this campus and away from this chick. I was heading to the station because I had an interview with Miley Cyrus. She'd been getting buck-wild crazy lately and had decided to talk to *Rumor Central*, but she was on a tight schedule. I needed to have skipped seventh period altogether, but my test was after school. Ms. Watson wasn't trying to hear it and told me if I missed that make-up test (I'd missed the original one because I had to go to Tampa to shoot an interview), I was going to take an F. And since I couldn't end up flunking and not graduating, I had to stay the whole time.

I got to my car in the parking lot, hit the remote to unlock it, and was just about to throw my purse in the backseat when I noticed my back tire on flat.

"You have *got* to be freaking kidding me," I mumbled. "Oh my God, what am I supposed to do?" I said, looking at my watch. I leaned down and touched the tire—not that I knew anything about tires, but I could tell that it was definitely completely flat.

"Ugh," I said kicking it, which only hurt my toe.

There was no way I had time to wait for AAA to come. I looked around the parking lot, trying to find the security guard, a bumbling pseudo-cop who did nothing but walk around looking like he was seven months pregnant with his stomach hanging over his too-tight pants. Of course, his worthless behind was nowhere to be found.

"Doggone it," I said. "What am I supposed to do?" I had exactly fifteen minutes to get to the station.

Finally, the rent-a-cop came rounding the corner. "Is there a problem?" he asked.

"Yeah, my tire is on flat," I said, pointing at my tire.

He leaned back, looked at it, and snorted. "It sure is."

"Can you help me change it?" I snapped.

"Well, changing tires isn't in my job description," he chuckled.

"What?" I said. "Are you for real?"

"I'm kidding, I'm kidding." He held up his hands defensively. "You teenagers have no sense of humor."

I wanted to tell him to try saying something funny and it might give me a reason to laugh, but because I needed him to hurry up and change the tire, I kept my mouth closed.

"Let me see here," he said, leaning down. "Yep, it's on flat."

Duh! "Can you help me change it?" I asked, trying to keep the exasperation out of my voice.

He walked around my BMW, inspecting it like he was at a car dealership or something.

"Oh, this one of those fancy-schmancy cars. Don't know what happened to a good ol' Toyota or a Honda. . . . I *know* how to change tires on those." He stopped right at the back of the car. "Don't you need some kind of special tools or something?"

"I don't know," I snapped. Did I look like I knew the first thing about tires? I didn't even feel like going at it with him. I looked at my watch again. I had twenty minutes before my interview and the station was exactly twenty minutes away.

"How long is it going to take you to change it?" I asked.

"Well." He kneeled, then cocked his head like he was studying the tire. "It'll take a good twenty or thirty minutes I'm guessing."

"Are you for real? You can't do it any faster?"

He glared at me like he didn't appreciate my tone.

He stood back up. "Or you can call AAA."

"I don't have time to wait on AAA," I protested.

He wiped his hands to get the dirt off from where he was kneeling. "Well, I don't know what to tell you, little lady. Do you want me to help you or not?"

"Ugh," I moaned.

"What's wrong?"

I looked up to see Bryce, his backpack slung across his shoulder. He was stopped just in front of my car.

"The little lady got a flat and it seems like she's a tad bit impatient," the security guard said.

Bryce let out a small chuckle. "Impatience is her middle name," he joked.

I didn't smile. I didn't need him thinking anything was funny.

"Hey," Bryce said, stepping over to me. "Chill out. What's wrong?"

"I need to be at the station in, like, ten minutes."

I looked at the keys dangling in Bryce's hands and, while riding with him was the last thing I wanted to do, right now I didn't have a choice. "Can you give me a lift to the station?"

"Um, well, I was about to go—"

"Look, I'm not trying to keep you from your little girl-friend," I said, cutting him off.

He turned his lips up. "I was saying I was about to go to practice. I was just coming to get my cleats out the car."

Right now, Bryce was my only hope since the parking lot was half empty. "Bryce, I'm sorry," I said. "I just really have to get to the station. Can you run me over there?"

"I guess I can let coach know that I'll be late," he said, looking back at the field.

"I'll vouch for you. Whatever I need to do. Just please?"

"All right, cool," he said. "Come on."

"You know you're not supposed to leave your car parked in the parking lot overnight," fake-cop yelled after me as Bryce and I darted to his car.

"I'll send AAA to come fix it and I'll come back after I'm done," I called back.

I didn't wait for him to reply as I jumped into Bryce's car.

We rode in silence before Bryce finally said, "Are you sure you're all right?"

"I'm just irritated," I said, turning to stare out of the window. I didn't like how Bryce always seemed to be there when I needed him. I was so over him and I didn't want him to start seeing himself as some kinda superhero savior or something. In fact, he didn't need to get it twisted. Yes, he'd been there for me on more than one occasion, but at the end of the day, I was still done with him.

"Are you irritated about your tire, or is it something more?"

I just looked out the window. I wasn't in the mood for small talk.

"Is it the stuff with Evian?" he asked.

I nodded, even though I didn't want to.

Bryce said, "Yeah, I see how she's milking this for all it's worth. I figured it had to be bugging you."

I was tripping because Bryce seemed to be the only one who got that and didn't think I was just overreacting.

"It is so frustrating because Evan is just playing it up. She's trying to bogart my territory. She just makes me sick."

"I know this doesn't mean anything to you," Bryce said, as he maneuvered off the freeway. "But can't nobody steal your shine."

I cut my eyes at him. "I know that," I said. I didn't want to tell him how it felt to hear him say that. "Can you just get me to the station? I can't be late."

That's all I needed from Bryce. A ride. That's all I *wanted* from Bryce. At least that was what I kept telling myself as he sped toward the station.

Chapter 20

I was so glad I didn't have to go live on the air today. I was so frazzled by the time Bryce dropped me off. Thank God that Miley was late, so I had a few minutes to spare. Then, the interview hadn't taken that long. Miley had shared some awesome stuff, put a few rumors to rest, and talked about what was next on tap for her. I couldn't wait for the interview to air.

Now that I'd had that out of the way, I needed to get my car situation taken care of. Well, I needed to call Travis and tell him to handle it. What was the use of having male relatives if they didn't handle stuff like this?

"So, you got me covered?" I asked my cousin.

He blew an exasperated breath. "You know I got you, but I don't want to hear any flak when I tell you to do something for me," he warned.

"Of course you won't," I said. *Yeah, right,* I really wanted to say.

"A'ight, I'll be by the station to pick you up after I get this taken care of."

"Thanks, cuz," I told him.

I hung up, did a few more things around my office, and

was just about to go talk to Tamara when I bumped right into Evian in the doorway of my office.

"Maya," she said, giving me a fake air kiss. I didn't return it.

"Evian, what's going on?" I looked around. "What are you doing back here? We don't have another interview, do we?"

She laughed as she looked to her left, then her right. "Oh, just searching around, seeing which one of these"—she leaned in and looked inside my office—"I want for my office."

"Excuse me?"

As if she needed to make sure I didn't miss a word, Evian looked directly at me. "Tamara told me to just pick a room." She looked directly at me. "*Any* room. And I'm kinda sorta feeling yours."

"You got me messed up," I found myself saying. "If you think you're moving in to my office, you'd better think again." Why would Evian even need an office? Surely, she was just saying something to get under my skin.

"Now, now," Evian said, wagging her finger. "Don't get testy. I don't like your office anyway because it's facing the west. I need sunshine coming in to my office."

"Why are you even getting an office?" I asked.

"Oh, you hadn't heard?" she said with a huge grin. "I need an office because I'm getting a show."

The look on my face must've told her that I had no idea because she continued with her cheesy grin. "They told me they'd be discussing it with you. I'd think you'd be happy for me, but Wade—"

"Who is Wade?" I asked, cutting her off.

She giggled again, sounding like a stupid broken mechanical doll. "Oh, I'm sorry. You know him as Mr. Hampton, the station manager. Well, Mr. Hampton had some fabulous ideas for my show."

"Really?" I folded my arms and glared at her. "So, *Wade* is giving input into your show?"

"Yep," she said, excitedly. "I'm so looking forward to all the stuff they have planned for me."

I paused, then said, "Evian, you know I don't have a beef with you, so as your friend—"

"Oh, you're my friend now?" she said, cutting me off.

"Yes, *as your friend*," I stressed, "I feel that I need to warn you that this is a rough business. It's only so long your kidnapping crisis will be front-page news."

"Oh, I know that." She waved me off. "But I also have many other talents and now that I have my own show, the world is about to see. What's the matter, Maya? Are you feeling threatened?"

That actually made me laugh. "Why in the world would I feel threatened by you?"

"I don't know. You tell me," Evian replied. "I was just wondering what it was about me that made you feel so insecure."

I faced her. "Trust and believe, I am not insecure. I see you up in here and I know what you're doing."

She glanced at me, losing her smile. "Tell me, Maya, what am I doing?"

"You're trying to parlay your fifteen minutes of fame into a career, but there was a reason *Miami Divas* got cancelled. It's because you other broads were boring."

"Wow," Evian said. "Us 'other broads.' "

She stepped closer to me. "Well, let me tell you something about *this* broad. This broad knows how to play the game and yes, I milked my kidnapping crisis as you said, for all it's worth and"—she looked at a piece of paper that I just now noticed she was holding—"judging by my new contract, it's worth a lot." She leaned back and looked in my office again. "On second thought, maybe I'll tell Tamara that I *do* want this office after all."

"Girl, bye!" I said.

The day she got my office would be the day Martians invaded the earth. It just wasn't happening.

"Well, I would love to sit here and continue to listen to your little jealous rant."

"I am not jealous of you."

"Call it what you want." She shifted her Birkin bag to her other arm. "But I must go. Hair and makeup are waiting for my promotional photo shoot. Holla at your girl," she said, using my tag line for my show as she strutted off.

I swear I felt like taking my Louboutin off and hurling it at the back of her head.

Instead, I made a beeline to Tamara's office. These people were on some kind of special drug if they were seriously considering letting Evian have a show, and I was definitely about to let them know how I felt about that outrageously stupid decision.

Chapter 21

"Maya, what are you doing?"

I ignored Kelley, Tamara's secretary, as I marched straight to her door. "You can't go in there. She's in there with Dexter."

"Yeah, I know," I said, not breaking my stride. "She's always in there with Dexter. But it's cool because I need to talk to both of them."

I flung the door open before Kelley could get out of her seat. She should've known by the look in my eyes, I was on a mission, and nothing, or no one, was going to stop me.

"Well, come on in, Maya," Tamara sarcastically said as she looked up from her computer. Dexter was sitting in front of her desk, his legs crossed, looking like a fashion reject in his super-tight skinny jeans and neon yellow T-shirt.

"What's up, Maya?" Dexter said with a smirk.

I ignored him and turned to Tamara. "Is it true that Evian is getting her own show?"

The two of them exchanged glances, and that gave me my answer.

Tamara pointed to the chair next to Dexter. "Maya, have a seat, please."

"I don't need to have a seat." I folded my arms defiantly. "Is it true that she's getting her own show?" I repeated.

Tamara looked at Dexter like she wanted him to jump in. He diverted his eyes so she looked back at me.

"Yes, she is," Tamara admitted.

"Are you freaking kidding me?" I yelled. "So you guys are really buying into this scam she has going?"

"We don't think it's a scam," Tamara said. "She has a unique story."

"No," I retorted, "she had something bad happen to her and she's trying to capitalize on it."

Dexter shrugged. "Whatever. So are we. The bottom line is, the girl is good."

"No, the girl is trying to parlay a tragedy into fifteen minutes of fame," I corrected.

"And it's working," Dexter added. "The show she was on was one of *Rumor Central*'s highest rated, and she's one of the most talked about people on TMZ."

"Really?" I said. "Nobody outside of Miami even knows who Evian is."

"I beg to differ," he said, taking a magazine and tossing it on the desk in front of me.

"What is that?"

"It's an article featuring Evian," he said.

I picked it up. "Oh, my God, this is *People*."

"Exactly," Dexter replied.

I stared at Tamara. "Evian is in *People* magazine?" I asked her. Yeah, I was definitely salty about that. *I* hadn't even made *People* magazine.

" 'Her harrowing story,' " I said, reading the headline. "Oh, give me a break! Like she's the first girl to ever get kidnapped."

"She *is* one of the few celebrities to get kidnapped and live to tell about it," Tamara said.

"She's not a celebrity," I snapped. "She's rich, yes. She hangs with celebrities, yes. But she's not a celebrity."

"When you were on *Miami Divas,* did you consider yourself a celebrity?" Tamara asked.

"Yes, but—"

"No buts. She is a celebrity and her story is interesting."

I couldn't believe Tamara, as smart as she had appeared to be, was falling for Evian's game.

"So, what will you do when the novelty has worn off?" I asked. "When nobody's interested in Evian's story any longer?"

"Good careers are built on stories of the moment. That's when you capitalize on them. Of course, we know we can't hype this up forever. This is just to jumpstart things," Tamara said.

"Right, we don't expect to ride it out forever," Dexter added. "But we need to hop on the wave and ride it till it fizzles."

"So, you're going to build a whole show around this foolishness?" I was still trying to wrap my mind around everything.

"Evian isn't the same person that was on *Miami Divas.* She has spunk, and now"—he tapped on his phone and held it out for me to see—"she has five hundred and twelve thousand followers on Instagram."

"What?" I said, snatching his phone. I only had five hundred thousand followers. How in the world had she surpassed me?

"So, we think now is the time to capitalize on her notoriety. Build a show around her," Tamara said. "And I don't understand what the issue is. It's not in competition to your show. It will be a completely different type of show. It's a reality show, following her day-to-day life. Think *Jersey Shore* or *Keeping Up With the Kardashians,* but with a twist because she'll go behind the scenes of her celebrity friends' homes."

My mouth dropped open in disbelief. It's not like she hung with Kanye, vacationed with Beyoncé. Really?

No amount of words could convince me that this was a good idea. "So, you're really going to go through with this?" I asked.

"You didn't want her on your show." Tamara shrugged, like this was all my fault. "So, we had to find a fit for her and we think this is perfect."

"Plus," Dexter added, "it's already done. We start filming next week."

"If *Miami Divas* didn't work, what makes you think this will?" I couldn't help but ask.

Tamara picked up a stack of papers and dropped them back on her desk. "These Q ratings, they tell us what's hot and what's not. And Evian is hot. So her show, *All American Princess,* debuts soon."

I wanted to threaten to quit. Tell them either her or me. But number one, I was under contract and number two, if they called my bluff, I'd be sick. So instead, I just said, "Well, let me go on record as warning you that you are making a big mistake and when it flops, I'll be the first one there to tell you I told you so."

I turned and stormed out the room.

Chapter 22

I was still fuming from my conversation with Tamara and Dexter, not to mention Evian's cockiness. I didn't know why she was so full of herself because I knew she didn't think she was going to push me out of my place as the go-to chick at WSVV. I don't even know what her stupid show was going to be about, but I knew it wouldn't hold a candle to *Rumor Central*.

Since *Miami Divas* was canceled, Evian must've taken some type of personality classes because she had definitely upped her game a notch, but she *still* wasn't in my same category.

"I think you should just let it go," Kennedi said as she lay across my bed, flipping through a magazine. Kennedi had just gotten in town a few hours ago and I'd literally spent the whole time complaining about Evian.

"No, this isn't sitting right with me," I said as I paced back and forth across my bedroom. "I don't want this chick to think she can get to me."

Sheridan shrugged. "Just let her have her fifteen minutes of fame. Her show isn't going to compete with yours anyway."

"Duh," I said, looking at her like she was crazy. "I know

that, but I don't understand how she can blow up like that almost overnight, all because she was kidnapped."

"Unh-unh," Kennedi said. She sat up on the bed. "The more I think about it, something about this isn't passing the smell test to me."

Both Sheridan and I stopped and turned to look at her.

"What do you mean?" I asked. Kennedi was usually the skeptical one, but she was often right on point.

She turned up her lips. "I don't know, it's just all too convenient if you ask me. Think about it." Kennedi crossed her legs and got in her thinking position—the one where her mind got to churning as she was trying to figure something out. "So this girl, who just literally faded into nowhere, has now popped back on the scene. Why? Because she was kidnapped. A kidnapping where she wasn't hurt, they didn't get any money, and then you, of all people, just so conveniently happened to discover her."

"It wasn't convenient," I said, trying to figure out where she was going with this. "I had to go digging, remember? We couldn't find her."

"Yeah, but somehow, Shay miraculously just happened to locate her. I mean, how hard did you really have to dig?" Kennedi asked. "Think about it. Did you ever see a GPS tracer? No, you just took her word. And who goes up to a drug-dealing kidnapper's house in a foreign country without a second thought? Somebody who's not really scared, that's who."

I stopped. I hadn't thought about that.

"Like I said, just too convenient," Kennedi replied.

"So what, you think this was some kind of setup or that Evian staged her own kidnapping?" Sheridan asked.

She shrugged. "Maybe, maybe not. But I am saying that something just doesn't seem right, and if I were you, before I went throwing in the towel, I'd figure out what it is."

"Oh, trust, I'm not throwing in the towel," I said.

Kennedi lay back down. "I would just try to figure out what's going on."

"And how do I do that?" I asked.

"I don't know." She started flipping through her magazine again. "You said Evian's brother's assistant was quite nosey. Why don't you go talk to her?"

"Yeah, right. If she works for them, no way she's going to give up any information."

"Aren't you the queen of getting information from people?" Sheridan asked.

"Well, yeah."

"Well, then get on your job," Kennedi said, waving her hand like she was tired of talking about this.

"Kennedi is right. If anybody can get that woman to talk, Maya Morgan can," Sheridan said.

I thought about what they were saying. Something didn't seem right and I needed to do exactly like Kennedi said and start digging. I was going to start with that assistant, but I knew I needed to play it real careful because Evian's family wasn't one to be messed with.

Chapter 23

I sat in my car, parked outside of Javid's corporate offices, hoping that Delana wasn't one of those workaholics who grabbed a sandwich at her desk and worked right through her lunch break. I'd called her office yesterday and her voice mail had said she was out to lunch from twelve to one, so I'd skipped my own lunch, trying to catch her as she left, but she'd never shown.

Still, I'd come back today, determined, that sooner or later, she would have to leave the building. I knew I was messing up because I'd gotten a text from Sheridan that we'd had a pop quiz in fourth period. Oh, well. There was nothing I could do about it now.

I pushed aside thoughts of how much trouble I was about to be in at school and glanced at the clock, trying to decide how much time I was going to give Delana today before I called this whole idea a bust. As soon as I looked down, I noticed a redheaded woman bounce out of the front door of the office building. I'd had to Google Delana to see what she looked like and thankfully, there was one picture online. (Like seriously, though, who only had one picture on Google?) Thankfully, there was no mistaking that bright red hair.

I hoped that Delana wasn't going to run errands through her whole lunch break and that she was actually planning to sit down and eat somewhere so that I could talk to her. But I was prepared to approach her wherever I needed to. Now, I didn't know exactly what I was going to say to her. But if I was lucky, maybe she'd get to rattling on about how Evian hadn't really been kidnapped, or had paid off the kidnappers or some other story.

I breathed a sigh of relief as Delana turned her little Ford Focus into the Chick-fil-A restaurant, whipped into a parking space, then made her way inside. I gave her a minute, and then I followed her in. I stood behind her and watched her order, before getting a lemonade and side salad.

Delana sat over in the corner and pulled out one of those sappy romance novels (she looked like one of those die-hard Harlequin readers).

I acted like I was passing her table to go find somewhere to sit and eat, but I stopped in front of her and said, "Delana?"

She looked at me, confused.

"Hey, girl. How are you?" I asked with a big, cheesy grin.

"I'm fine. And you?" She smiled warmly, even though it was clear she had no clue who I was.

"I'm Maya, I'm a friend of Evian's. I met you at one of their company functions," I said.

"Oh, yeah," she said.

It was almost kinda funny because I'd never met this woman before, but she was smiling and nodding like she was recalling our meeting.

"Are you eating alone?" I asked.

"Well, ah . . ."

I sat down before she could finish. "Good. I hope you don't mind me sitting here, joining you. I'm just going to wolf this down because I only have about ten minutes."

That seemed to put her at ease. I guess she felt she could give me ten minutes because she closed her novel.

"I just left Evian," I said. "We had a major test today. I finished mine early and came to grab something to eat."

"Oh, okay."

I still didn't know exactly what I was looking for, but something about this woman told me if there was some dirt to be known, she knew it. But I knew I needed to play my cards just right.

"I sure do love your hair color," I told her. "Did you dye it?"

She grinned proudly as she fluffed her big ringlets. "Girl, no. I was born with this natural head full of red hair."

"Wow." I wanted to tell her she might want to make sure her brown roots weren't showing before she went lying to people about her hair color. "Well, it's very pretty."

"Thank you." She took a bite of her chicken sandwich. "So, how do you know Evian again?" she asked after she'd swallowed her food.

"I'm really good friends with her," I replied. "The whole family, in fact. She is always raving about you, talking about what a great assistant you are."

"Really?" She looked at me in shock.

"Yep. In fact, her whole family is always talking about you and how they'd be lost without you." I knew I was laying it on thick, but I needed to put her at ease so she'd become the chatterbox that I knew she was.

"Well, that's nice to know," she said.

I took a bite of my salad, then made more small talk. Finally, as I was nearing my ten-minute mark, I said, "Isn't it great that Evian is getting her own show? I told her this morning how proud of her I was."

Delana smiled. "We all are proud of her."

I shook my head in fake admiration. "I'm telling you, when that girl sets her mind to do something, she gets it done."

"Who are you telling," Delana said, slurping up her lemonade. "That whole family is like that."

"I know." I leaned in and lowered my voice. "I mean, when Evian told me that she'd go to any lengths to get her chance at fame, I thought she was kidding."

Delana lost her smile. "So you know what she did?" she asked.

I looked around like I was trying to make sure no one was listening. "Shhh. Only a few of us know." Delana seemed shocked as I continued. "I'm sure Clinton was not pleased about it. Evian told me that he was pretty mad about everything."

Delana looked around as well. "You know he wasn't. He couldn't believe she would have everyone scared like that. But Evian has always been a little hothead." She laughed. "Boy, if he had gone searching for her in Cancun, it would not have been pretty."

"How did he find out that she had faked the kidnapping? Did Evian come clean?"

Delana suddenly stopped, looked at me, and frowned. "Wait a minute, don't I know you? Were you on *Miami Divas* with Evian?"

Dang, I had been hoping to make it through this whole conversation without being recognized.

"Yes." I nodded, but only because I knew there was no way around it.

"Maya Morgan, right?" she asked.

"Yes."

She completely lost her smile. In fact, fear spread all across her face. "Yeah, um, I gotta go." She stood and started gathering up her stuff.

"Wait, what did I do?" I said.

"Oh my God. Oh my God," she kept muttering. "I can't believe this."

"What's going on?" I tried to stop her as she moved away from the table.

"Look, I don't need any drama," she said. "Evian can't stand you. I don't know what you're trying to do, but please don't let anyone know that you talked to me. Mr. Javid doesn't play that. He's very protective of his little sister."

"Of course, I won't tell anyone anything. But please, just tell me, did Evian make up her story about being kidnapped?"

"You have got to be kidding if you think I'm about to say a word to you." She snatched her arm away. "Good-bye."

She stomped out of the restaurant, and I felt like I was back at the beginning of plan A.

Chapter 24

The sight on my TV made me sick to my stomach. How in the world had Evian gone from being a nobody to having her own show, complete with all the bells and the whistles?

All American Princess flashed across the screen.

"You've got to be kidding me," I mumbled. Not only had they rushed production, but now, it was on the air right after my show. I'd taped my show yesterday and at no time had anyone told me Evian's show had been taped too and would air after mine.

I wanted to throw a brick right at my fifty-two-inch TV.

"What's up, everybody? It's your girl Evian, and I'm back on the block and ready to rock." She danced across the screen, looking like a bootleg *Real Housewives of Atlanta* introduction.

I rolled my eyes. She couldn't come up with a better corny saying than that? I *did* feel some kind of way about the jazzy music and sweet graphics she had. I couldn't believe they were going to make her show look better than mine.

"Thanks for peeping into my life," she said into the camera. If this is supposed to be a reality show following her life, why was she talking to the camera like she was hosting some-thing? Oh yeah, probably because she was bitin' off me.

"Today we've got an exclusive. We're getting up close and personal with Tyrese. Yes, that's right. As you know, this *All American Princess* is well-connected and Tyrese is taking us to his crib."

What?! I wanted to scream. I'd been trying to get an in-terview with Tyrese for months!

"But first it's that time for *Talking It Up With Evian* and I am pleased to introduce my panel who will be joining me each week as we discuss some of Miami's hottest topics. They're known as the 'It Clique' around town, but I just call them my girls."

The camera shifted to a long table and I almost passed out when I saw Sheridan sitting at the end.

"First up, you know her as the daughter of the phenome-nal Glenda Matthews, but Sheridan Matthews is a diva in her own right. A former star of the *Miami Divas* along with yours truly, she's Miami's resident good girl, with a hint of bad."

Evian winked her eye at the camera, and Sheridan gig-gled, looking like a stupid second-grader.

"Next to her is *my* BFF, my ride or die, my road dog Shay Turner, daughter of Jalen Turner. You know him as the NBA three-time-world-championship center of the Miami Heat."

Shay raised her hand in the air. "Woo, woo!"

How incredibly ghetto, I thought.

"And back from a hiatus is none other than the flamboy-ant, the always-rocking-it Mr. Bali Fernandez."

I almost didn't recognize Bali because his brown hair was now deep blond and swooped down in his face with an asymmetrical cut. When had he gotten back? Why had no-body said anything to me? Those were all my former *Miami Divas* costars.

And so now they were going to try to be my competi-tion? This was all about revenge, pure and simple. They were trying to pay me back because I had gotten a show and they hadn't. I looked up to see Travis standing over me. I turned around and cut my eyes at him. He was actually trying not to giggle.

"Is their show any good?" he asked, trying to stifle his laughter.

"Of course it isn't."

He glanced over at the clock. "And you can determine that in the first five minutes?"

"I can determine that," I snapped, "because of the busters they have on it. I don't even know what they were talking about—some celebrity gossip. They're just bitin' off me. They couldn't even be original." I slammed the TV off. I was not only aggravated by the show and Sheridan, but Delana's words had been bugging me all night. She'd been about to let something slip. Something major. And although she hadn't, it had just made me even surer that this whole thing was fishy.

"So, you didn't know Sheridan was gonna be on the show?" Travis asked.

I shook my head. "No wonder Sheridan was avoiding me when I called her earlier. She knew she was a traitor." I grabbed my purse. "Unh-unh. I'm about to tell her about herself."

"Where are you going?" Travis asked, following me out of the family room.

I marched through the kitchen toward the garage. "I'm about to go over to your girl's house."

"Oh, I'm not about to miss this," Travis said, grabbing his baseball cap off the counter and following me out.

Fifteen minutes later, we were pulling up into Sheridan's circular driveway. Since I knew the code, I punched it in and made my way on inside. I banged on the door.

Sheridan came and opened it, looking all innocent. "Hey, girl, what's going on?"

"You tell me," I said, stomping past her.

"What's up, Travis?" she spoke. The two of them had dated a few months ago, despite the fact that I'd warned them against it. And since Travis was a pretty boy and fresh meat at our school, all the girls wanted him. It didn't take him long to cheat on Sheridan, and that had caused major drama. But I wasn't here for that.

"How are you?" Travis asked her as he followed me in.

"I'm cool. What's up with y'all?"

So, she really was going to continue and try to play me left?

"Nothing. I'm just along for the show," he said.

"What show?" Sheridan asked, closing her front door. Sheridan lived in this gigantic house all by herself. Well, her two aunts were supposed to be here with her, but they were always traveling, living off Sheridan's mother's money. Ms. Matthews, a Grammy-winning singer and actress, had wanted to keep Sheridan away from Hollywood, so she'd hired relatives to keep an eye on Sheridan. But she must not have known her relatives well because they took her money and let Sheridan do whatever she wanted, which was just fine with Sheridan.

"How could you do that?" I said, facing her. "You're such a traitor."

Sheridan rolled her eyes. "How am I a traitor?"

"You're really on Evian's show?"

She paused, shifting like she would really rather not have this conversation.

"Why didn't you tell me?" I demanded when she still didn't answer.

"Because I knew you would react just like this."

"How are you going to go on her show?"

Sheridan crossed her arms and raised an arched eyebrow. "When's the last time you invited me on *yours*?"

"So that's what this is about? My BFF goes on the competition's show as payback?"

"How 'bout this ain't got nothing to do with you?" Sheridan said. "Remember I was on TV, too. We all were, so it's something we all enjoy doing. Now you had an opportunity that you took, basically just throwing us to the wind."

"Wow," I said, taking a step back. I knew they were mad about me getting my own show, but I really thought Sheridan had gotten over it. "So, you're still holding a grudge?"

Sheridan let out a long sigh. "I have gotten over it. I don't have any beef with you about the way you did us behind *Miami Divas*. I get it. Yeah, I was salty for a minute, but at the end of the day, I get it. I understand, just like I feel like you should. This was an opportunity for me to get back on TV so I took it."

"And you didn't care who it hurt."

Travis was looking back and forth between us like he was in a Ping-Pong match.

"Do you hear yourself?" Sheridan asked. "What did you tell me when you started *Rumor Central*? It's not personal; it's business."

"How long have you been knowing you were going to be on her show?" I asked.

She looked away like she really didn't want to answer. "About two weeks."

"Wow," I said. "And at no time, did you feel like you needed to say, 'Hey, by the way, I'm starring on Evian's show now.' "

"No, because I didn't want to hear your mouth because I knew all Maya Morgan would care about is Maya Morgan." She glared at me defiantly.

"Just wow," I said. "Glad to know where we really stand." I couldn't even stand to be in the same room with her. "Come on, Travis," I said, stomping back toward the front door.

"I can't believe you're being so foul about this!" Sheridan called out after me.

I wasn't even trying to hear her as I swung the door open

and speed-walked to my car. Travis caught up with me just as I started up the car.

"You know you wrong," he said.

"Shut up, Travis."

He shrugged. "You are because Sheridan didn't do anything different to you than you did to her." He slid his shades on. "The difference is Maya Morgan can dish it, but she can't seem to take it."

Chapter 25

I was going to have a good night. That's what I told myself as I took a final survey of myself in my full-length mirror. I was looking tight (as usual) in my long burnt-orange Vera Wang gown. I was determined to exhale and let all my stress go. I'd been worked up behind Evian for the past few weeks, and it was time I just let that go and get back to doing me.

I was a presenter at the *Hype* magazine Teen Choice Awards tonight, and I was looking forward to putting aside any thought of Evian and her stupid show, Sheridan back-stabbing me, and the fact that it hadn't been until three days ago that I'd realized I didn't even have a date for tonight. I'd been so consumed with the show that I had let this slip up on me.

I ended up doing what I normally do when I find myself in a bind. I called Alvin. And I almost fell over when he told me he didn't know if he could go because he and Marisol had a date. But he wanted me to believe that she wasn't his girl. If she wasn't, then why did she take priority over me?

Lucky for Alvin, he called me back before I could get in touch with another guy and told me that he was able to re-arrange his schedule and go. I almost told him don't worry about it, but I knew that I would have fun with Alvin, he wouldn't be sweating me all night long, and if I saw a cutie that I really wanted to pick up, Alvin wouldn't give me a hard time.

"Come on, honey," my mom said, appearing in my doorway. "Your boyfriend is downstairs waiting. You've had that poor boy down there for twenty minutes already. And Travis is grilling him like crazy."

"Mom, I don't know how many times I have to tell you that Alvin is not my boyfriend," I said, grabbing my Brahmin clutch and heading down the stairs.

"Well, then I don't see why you couldn't let Travis escort you. You know he's never been exposed to things like this."

"Ewwww," I said. "Have my cousin as my date? As if."

My mom had lost her mind. I would not be on the red carpet with my cousin as my date. And what was her fascination with Travis lately anyway? He'd taught her how to Dougie now all of sudden, he was supernephew?

She must've known to drop that because just as we reached the bottom of the staircase, she said, "You look amazing. But you are Liza Morgan's daughter so what else would one expect?"

"You do look gorgeous," Alvin said, approaching me. "But I'd expect nothing less."

"Dude, you are so corny." Travis laughed.

"Take note, young buck, take note," Alvin told him.

We laughed as we said our good-byes, then made our way out to Alvin's car—a shiny red corvette. He may have been a nerd, but Alvin knew how to step up his game when necessary. Whenever he took me somewhere, this is what we rolled in, and he cleaned up very nice. Tonight, he was looking fab in a tuxedo jacket with a T-shirt. It was just enough class and just enough casual for him to look like he belonged on the arm of Maya Morgan.

It took us thirty minutes to get to the facility, but thankfully Alvin had me in a good mood, laughing and talking as I made my way to my reserved seating.

Before I could sit down, a young girl with a headset on her ears came over to me and said, "Miss Morgan, here's your script for today." She handed me a stack of index cards wrapped inside a piece of paper. "We'll need you backstage ten minutes before your presentation. Someone will come get you when we're ready," she said.

"Who am I presenting with?" I asked, unwrapping the piece of paper she had just given to me. I hoped it was someone like Usher or Nick Cannon. I almost fell over in my stilettos when I saw the name on my paper.

"Evian Javid? Are you freaking serious?" I said, waving the paper at the girl. "I'm presenting with her?"

The poor girl looked horrified. "I-I'm sorry. I don't have anything to do with that. They just told me to come bring it to you."

I turned to Alvin. "Can you believe this bull?"

Just then I heard, "So I would guess that means today is your lucky day." Evian was grinning like she'd won the lotto as she came up on the side of me.

I ignored Evian and turned back to the girl. "Why am I presenting with her?"

The young girl shrugged. "I don't know. I just pass out the scripts. Someone will be here to get you." She scurried away before I could go off any more.

"So, we get to do our thing together," Evian sang. "Isn't that fab?"

I just looked at her, rolled my eyes, and went to my seat. She giggled at her date, who was none other than Hollywood heartthrob Lance Malone. Seeing that gave me pause, but I couldn't let her know that I was fazed by it at all. Though I definitely couldn't understand how she'd managed to snag a gem like Lance.

She draped her arm though Lance's and headed down the aisle behind me. She stopped in front of my row. "Well, Maya. I'll see you on stage. Lance got us some great seats right there," she said, pointing three rows up.

"Oh, I don't think so," I mumbled as she walked off. "I'm going to find someone to move our seats." I stood and was just about to step over Alvin and make my way out to the aisle.

Alvin put his hand on mine and settled me down. "Come on, Maya, chill out. People are already starting to look." He motioned to his right as some woman was discreetly trying to hold up her iPhone. I'm sure she was hoping to capture a fight.

"You're right," I said. "Let me pull it together." I sat back in my seat and waited for the show to start, but my mood had been soured—once again, thanks to Evian.

When the young girl came back and told me, "They're ready for you," I knew that I had to pull it together. This was televised so the last thing I needed to do was be on stage letting my emotions get the best of me.

I made my way backstage and both Evian and Lance were already back there, laughing and talking with some people.

The host, comedian and actor Kevin Hart, came over to me first. "Well, if it isn't Maya Morgan," he said, shaking my hand. "Let me make sure I don't make you mad, because I know you'll have it turn up on me," he said with his little signature laugh.

I didn't even get a chance to respond before Evian barged into our conversation.

"You are so silly," she said as she approached us. "Nice to meet you, I'm Evian Javid." She shook his hand. "I'm a big fan."

Evian was so low-class. The first rule of thumb about being a celebrity was you had to act like one—and that meant not getting all starry-eyed around the stars.

"Where do I know you from?" he asked, studying her.

"The reality show *All American Princess*," she replied.

Kevin smiled at her. "Oh yeah, you're that cute girl that has that new little show."

"Um, cute? I wouldn't say that," she said, giving him a flirtatious wink. "Try beautiful." She was completely disrespecting Lance, who was standing over in a corner talking to someone. I started to yell at him to come get his girl!

Kevin's eyes roamed up and down her. "That you are."

"And my show definitely isn't little. In fact, it's about to be one of the biggest things on TV. Watch and see." With that, she bounced back over to Lance.

Kevin watched her as she walked off, completely turning his attention away from me. It took everything in my power not to go off on his little behind, but since I didn't need the drama, I just turned and walked away.

I stood over to the side trying to compose myself until they called for us to come forward. The music started playing as we made our way onto the stage. I stepped on the stage first and then Evian just bumped right on past me and went to the podium.

"Hello, Miami," she said, excitedly. "I am Evian Javid, host of *All American Princess* and this is Maya Morgan, she—"

No, this slug wasn't about to try to introduce me!

I stepped up. "And *I* am the host of the number-one-rated show, *Rumor Central*." The teleprompter began rolling. The way the script was set up, there was a section for Evian to read, and then a section for me to read. We were supposed to go back and forth. Since Evian's name was listed first, I stepped aside to let her speak.

"We're here to present the Newsmaker of the Year Award," she began. "This award is given to an artist who is constantly in the news. This person can be an actor, musician, or philanthropist," she continued reading, even though it was clear my name was above that line. As soon as she took a breath, I jumped in.

"This person is someone who is always making head-lines—whether good or bad," I read.

Before I could get out the next sentence—which again, had my name on it, Evian spoke.

"They are the ones who are constantly being talked about."

I kept my smile as I leaned toward the mic. "The ones who are making all the headlines. Who—"

She leaned in and cut me off. "Who we love to talk about. Who we—"

I'd had enough. I kept my smile as I said, "You do see that has my name on it?"

"Excuse me." She let out an uncomfortable laugh as she stood up straight.

"I'm supposed to read that," I said, pointing at the teleprompter. I know it was incredibly unprofessional, but I was so sick and tired of Evian that I had literally had all I could take. "See, my name above those lines means I read. It doesn't mean for you to keep reading. The names are there for a reason."

Evian looked momentarily shocked, then leaned in like she was trying to get a closer look at the teleprompter. "I guess it does say your name." She looked out at the audience and let out a small laugh. "Sorry, I don't have my contacts in—they mess with my mink lashes." She batted her eyes. Several people laughed, but I didn't see anything funny. "Anyway," she continued, "I know these people don't care who reads what, so let's just get the winner announced. So the nominees are—"

"No, ma'am. I don't think so," I said, cutting her off. I snatched the envelope with the winner's name from her.

"Really, Maya?" she whispered as I stepped in front of her.

I ignored her and continued reading the teleprompter. "And the nominees for Newsmaker of the Year are, Miley Cy—"

She snatched the envelope back and took over. "Miley Cyrus, Usher, Justin Bieber—"

I snatched the envelope right back from her. We went back and forth grabbing the oversized envelope, both of us refusing to let go.

"Give it here," she said.

"Are you really doing this?" I replied. "You are so janky!" As it dawned on me that we were actually on stage, in front of two thousand people, I quickly came back to my senses. I let the envelope go and Evian stepped back victoriously—then stumbled right over her gown. I watched in horror as she screamed and toppled to the floor.

The crowd was just as stunned as I heard several gasps and people jumped to their feet. I needed to do something and do it, now!

I stuck my hand out to help Evian up. She glared at me with evil eyes. "Just go with it," I whispered through my smile. "We look like idiots and need to clean this up."

As the confused crowd stared at us, I stepped to the podium. "Gotcha," I said with a huge grin. "We're good, aren't we? You wanted reality drama, we gave it to you. Right, Evian?"

Evian dusted herself off as she glared at me and forced a fake smile. I guess looking out at the crowd told her we needed to do something to clean this up because she said, "Yep, all part of the act . . ."

As the crowd started applauding, I felt like I'd proven my point with Evian, and cleaned up any mess that might've been brewing. That's why I tossed my curls over my shoulder, stepped back to the microphone, and continued, "So, now back to our regularly scheduled program. The winner of Newsmaker of the Year is Miley Cyrus!"

As Miley made her way to the stage, Evian shot me daggers and somehow I got the feeling our battle had just intensified. But I wasn't worried. If anything, I'd just added my name to the newsmaker list, and after all was said and done, I'd probably be the one up here accepting this award next year. And I would take great pleasure in watching Evian watch me win.

Chapter 26

After that disaster at the Teen Choice Awards, I didn't care if I ever saw Evian again. In fact, it was probably best I didn't see her because I couldn't be held responsible for what I might do. That's why I took the long way around when I arrived at the station. I saw her car parked out front and I went around through the back simply because I didn't want to pass her office because there was no telling what I might do if I saw her, as she probably was itching to start a fight with me. So I needed to play it cool, and for right now that meant staying clear of her. Trust, I wasn't scared of her. I just didn't need her bringing me down any further than she already had.

I had just slung my purse over my shoulder and was going up the back walkway to WSVV when I noticed Evian talking with a guy who looked very familiar.

I pushed up against the wall so that they couldn't see me. Was that—? No, that wasn't the guy that she had disappeared with, but he sure did look familiar.

I told myself that it was just my imagination looking for something, but then I saw the distressed look on Evian's face and I knew something wasn't right. I couldn't hear what they were saying, but I saw her shuttle him away. He looked agitated, but he did go to his car and instead of going back in the building, Evian walked around to the parking lot to her own car.

I was just about to leave, but I stopped myself. I wasn't going to mind my own business. My gut was in overdrive for a reason. I needed to see what in the world they were up to. I waited until Evian got in her car then I raced back around, jumped in mine, and began following them. She was right behind the guy and I stayed about two car lengths behind her.

"Where is she going?" I mumbled.

I followed them to T.G.I. Friday's, where they went inside. *Why would she be getting something to eat?* I thought.

I could see the hostess sit them at a table in the back corner. Man, I would've given anything to be able to hear what they were talking about. Even still, I eased into a booth at the bar and just sat, waited, and watched as I struggled to figure out why this guy looked familiar. Whatever they were talking about had Evian agitated and worked up. Then he pulled out his phone and began punching the screen, but she stopped him, and he eased the phone down. The next thing I knew, she pulled out her purse, got out her checkbook, and wrote a check.

Why in the world is she giving this man money? I thought. The waitress came over and took their order. It was obvious that Evian wasn't trying to eat, but he seemed to be ordering up a storm. As soon as the waitress walked off, Evian threw the check at him, said something, and then raced out. My first instinct was to follow her, but then something said he was the one I'd needed to be getting information from. I sat for a minute trying to make sure he wasn't anybody who knew me since he looked so familiar. I couldn't place him, so I could only hope that he didn't know me. So, finally, I made my move.

"Hey, handsome, is this seat taken?" I said, walking up just as the waitress set a salad down in front of him.

He looked me up and down, a big cheesy grin across his face. "It is now," he said. He pointed to the seat. "Please, sit."

"Sorry." I slid into the seat across from him. "I don't mean to be forward, but I'm a little bummed. My boyfriend stood me up and I'm going to dump him. I saw your girlfriend leave and she seemed kind of angry, so I thought maybe I could buy you a drink."

He put his napkin on the table. "*You* buy *me* a drink? You don't get a girl who offers to pay for stuff often." Even though it was a little choppy, I was surprised at how well he spoke English. I had the strangest feeling he spent a lot of time in the States.

"Oh, I'm an equal-opportunity woman," I said with a sexy smile. Trying to pretend I was attracted to him was hard because he actually came across as kind of slimy, which made my skin itch.

"Oh, you're a woman, huh?" he replied.

I motioned up and down my body. "Don't I look it?"

"You sure do." He took a bite of his salad, stuffing a forkful of lettuce into his mouth. "Well, that's not my girlfriend," he replied with his mouth full. Just gross. "She's just a girl I have a business transaction with."

"Oh. What kind of business are you in?"

He stopped. "You sure ask a lot of questions."

"Hey, chill," I said. "I was just making small talk. Anything to keep my mind off of my jerk of a boyfriend."

He leaned forward, a huge green piece of lettuce stuck in his two front teeth. "Well, I definitely am the one to keep your mind off of that."

I smiled even though he made me sick to my stomach. I eyed his phone. That was going to give me the answers I needed. But how in the world could I get it? The napkin he'd thrown on the table had covered it, but I was sure when he got up to leave he'd get his phone.

Finally, I said, "What you drinking now?"

"Just a root beer."

"How about I order us some drinks?"

"Are you old enough to drink?"

"My ID says that I am."

"That's what I'm talking about."

I reached out like I was ready to take his hand and I knocked over his extra-large root beer and it went tumbling straight into his lap.

"Man!" he said, jumping up.

"Oh, I am so sorry!"

"*¡Chica estúpida!*"

"You want me to go get some napkins?" I said, acting horrified. "Or you can get cleaned up. The restroom is right there."

He seemed really irritated. "I'll be right back," he said as he went to the restroom.

That was my cue. As soon as I saw him step inside, I grabbed his phone, which was open on the home screen. *What idiot doesn't lock their phone these days?* I scrolled through his phone log. Evian's number was on there several times. I whipped my phone out, took a quick picture of his call log screen so I could have the numbers to look up later, and then kept scrolling to see if there was anything else. Nothing was giving me a clue, and then I saw it. A picture of Carson. This guy and Carson were drinking and holding up beers as they toasted the camera. So they knew each other? But where did I know him from? And what was this guy's connection to Evian?

I placed his phone back under the napkin and hightailed it out of there. I had been determined before to find out what Evian was up to, but now, I was on a mission and I wouldn't rest until I got my questions answered.

Chapter 27

Evian may have had everyone else fooled, but Kennedi was right, this wasn't adding up. It was one thing to capitalize on a "tragedy," but it was like this opportunity was falling into her lap and she was just taking it and running with it. I was definitely starting to agree with Kennedi. I smelled a setup.

But I didn't have the slightest idea where to begin in trying to put all the pieces of this puzzle together. I didn't know how I was going to get to the bottom of what was really happening. I'd gotten nowhere with Delana. But I knew if anyone could help, Alvin could.

I had learned my lesson about just popping over, so I'd called and he knew I was on my way. Even still, my heart quickened as I waited for him to answer the door. I don't know why I felt twinges of jealousy when I thought about Alvin with someone else. He was a geek with a capital G. He was my friend and really cool, but it's not like I had any romantic interest in him, so I don't know why who he was dating bugged me. But it did.

"Well, if it isn't my princess," Alvin said, opening the door and giving me a big hug.

"I keep trying to tell you, boy. I'm the queen." I winked at him as I sashayed past him into the house.

He closed the door and motioned for me to follow him back to his bedroom. The first time he'd done that, I thought he was some kind of pervert, but I'd since learned that was where he did all his work, so it was no biggie.

"So, what's this top-secret mission that you can't tell me about over the phone?"

"I could. But I knew if you saw me in person, there was no way you could tell me no." I flashed a smile at him and he shook his head.

"You think those big brown eyes can get you whatever you want, don't you?"

"Yes," I said, playfully batting my eyelashes.

He laughed as he sat down in the chair at his desk. "You don't have to try and con me, baby. I got your back no matter what."

"Good," I said, putting my Chanel bag down on his dresser. "Then, let's get to work."

"So, what is it you want me to do online now?" he asked.

"How do you know I want you to do something online? Maybe I just want to talk to you." I wiggled my foot in his direction. "Maybe I just want a foot massage."

"Oh, my pleasure," he said, scooting his rolling chair toward me.

I pulled my foot back. "Boy, quit playing. You know I need your super tech skills."

"Of course, I know that," he said, laughing as he rolled back over to the computer. "So, what you need?"

I eased up behind him. "I need you to hack into someone's cell phone account."

He sat back, acting like he was appalled at my request. "Oooh, you do know that's illegal, right?"

"And? When has that ever stopped you before?"

Alvin grinned. "You're right about that. What's the phone number?" he asked, tapping on his keyboard.

I pulled out my phone and began scrolling until I got to Evian's number. "It's 786-333-4612."

"Okay, give me a minute. Is there a time frame you're looking for?"

I thought about it for a minute, before saying, "Let me do the last thirty days. That should cover our time in Cancun."

"All right, give me a minute."

I looked around his house as he went to work. At least he'd opened some blinds and let some light in. When I'd first come here, he'd kept the room dark. There was all kinds of computer equipment and gaming stuff. Stacks of comic books sat in the corner. Marvel comics and superhero posters hung on the walls. Since I'd met him, at least he'd upgraded from his twin bed and gotten a queen-sized bed with a grown man's comforter (he used to have an Avengers comforter). There was no way, at the time I met him, I would've thought we could ever be friends. Kennedi had a friend who had hooked me up with Alvin to help me out with some computer issues.

"Okay, I'm in," Alvin announced.

"Boy, you are some kind of good," I said, giving him a hug from behind.

"And one day, you're going to realize what a good guy I am. I just hope it's not too late." He flashed a knowing smile.

The thing I loved about Alvin was he'd make those comments, then keep it moving, so there was never time for any uncomfortable air to hang.

"What are you looking for?" he asked as I began scanning her call log over his shoulder.

"I don't know." I shrugged.

"I don't know how to help you then." He studied the screen with me. "She had a lot of international numbers on the sixteenth."

I thought for a moment. "That's around the time that she was kidnapped. Matter of fact, she went missing on the sixteenth."

"What time was that?"

My mind raced as I tried to recall the time we were on the beach. "It had to be pretty late, like one in the morning."

"Yeah, these calls were pretty late," he said. "Four a.m. Even six a.m."

"Okay, that's after she went missing." I rubbed my head, trying to think. "And who is she calling?" I asked.

"786-959-3399."

"That number sounds familiar." I pulled my phone out and began scrolling through it. "That's Shay's number! So she was calling Shay when she was supposed to be kidnapped." I paused as my mind raced. "But Shay said she hadn't heard from her. This isn't making sense. Maybe this was some kind of time delay."

Alvin shook his head. "Nah, these times are usually on point. And look, since she's gotten back, she's been getting a lot of calls from that same international number that she called on the seventeenth, the day after she was kidnapped." He pointed to the screen. It was the same number popping up over and over. None of the calls were that long.

"Let me see your phone," I told Alvin.

"For what?" he asked.

"I want to call that number."

"Girl, do you know how much it costs to call international numbers?"

"Boy, be quiet. It's not like you can't afford it." Alvin had sold a patent to a large corporation and although he'd never told me for how much, I think it was definitely a lot of money.

He huffed, then said, "Let me do it." He put the phone on speaker, then punched in the number and waited for it to ring.

"Hello," the voice answered on the second ring.

I didn't say anything as I strained to make out the familiar voice.

"Hello. Who is this?" the voice repeated when we didn't answer.

The guy sounded so familiar. *Is that . . . ? No, it couldn't be. Why would Evian be calling him?*

"Ask him who it is," I said, pushing Alvin's shoulder.

He looked at me, confused, but said, "Who is this?"

"This is Miguel. Who you calling?"

Alvin held the phone for a second, then said, "Sorry, Miguel. I have the wrong number." He hung up the phone and looked at me. "It was Miguel. Do you know him?"

I frowned. Maybe my mind was just creating stuff.

"Nah, where is that number coming from? Cancun?"

Alvin tapped his screen. "Okay, it's a Cancun phone number, but it says the call is originating here in Miami," Alvin said.

"This isn't making sense. Why would someone be calling her from there?"

"Maybe she met a man," Alvin said.

"The girl was kidnapped. When would she have time to meet a man?"

"I guess your Spidey senses are going into overdrive?"

"They sure are. Thanks, Alvin," I said, giving him a quick kiss on the forehead.

"That's all that I get?"

"What else do you want?" I joked as I grabbed my purse.

"You." He wasn't smiling when he said that.

"Bye, boy," I said, playfully pushing his head. "I'll call you later."

I grabbed my purse and headed out. So Evian was meeting up with a strange guy who knew Carson, and calling someone named Miguel.

I opened the door and crawled into my front seat. I needed to get home because it was getting late and I had school in the morning. But I knew I wouldn't get any sleep tonight. I was getting close to uncovering the truth about Evian; I could feel it in my gut. And I couldn't wait.

Chapter 28

This was definitely what I needed to lift my mood. I had temporarily set aside all thoughts of Evian and was in my element being interviewed by entertainment reporter Jay Bee for the *Tom Joyner Morning Show*. He was doing this whole entertainment piece on "Young, Black and Fabulous," and I was happy to be the focus of his interview.

We were sitting in Che LeReu, on Miami's South Beach. It was a gorgeous day and the whole atmosphere was on point.

"So, Miss Morgan," Jay said. We'd only been doing our interview for five minutes, but I could tell he was already enamored with me. Then again, who wouldn't be? "What is it that you think makes everyone want to share their innermost secrets with you?"

"Well, I think it's just my personality," I began. "I'm a good listener and I really . . ." before I could finish my sentence, the front door of the restaurant swung open and a loud commotion followed.

Both Jay and I turned toward the noise. It was a cameraman backing in the door and several lights were around him as a crowd of people surrounded him. I almost fell over when

I saw what they were shooting. Evian sashayed in first. Behind her was Sheridan, Shay, and Bali. The look on my face spoke volumes because Jay looked at me, then looked at them and said, "Wait, aren't those the former *Miami Divas*?" I didn't reply just as Evian spotted me.

"Maya!" she said, waving in my direction. Why she kept trying to act like we were cool was beyond me. She bounced her little behind over toward me with Shay and Bali right behind her. Sheridan was smart enough to stay her butt right there by the door.

"Girl, what's going on? What are you doing here?" Evian asked. She was so fake. She probably followed me here or checked my publicity calendar so she could barge into my interview.

When I didn't speak, Jay said, "Hi, I'm Jay Bee with the *Tom Joyner Morning Show* and we're doing an interview."

"So, as you can see," I said, finally speaking up, "we're a little busy."

"No need to get all nasty," Shay said. All of them were camera ready. Shay was looking her usual ghetto-fabulous self in her twenty-six-inch blond weave, her BCBG catsuit, and stilettos (but, though I'd never in a million years tell her, I was digging that Birkin bag). Bali was over the top, too, in his Rock and Republic skinny jeans and boyfriend jacket with the sleeves rolled up. Even Sheridan looked cute in a silver silk maxi dress.

"Yeah, Maya," Bali added. "You don't need to get testy with us. If this talented journalist would rather waste his time talking with you instead of getting the *real* scoop on the *All American Princess* and her crew," he said, "who are we to stop him?"

I wanted to tell him that's exactly what he was doing, but before I could say anything, Jay actually smiled. "What kind of scoop?"

"Oh, we're about to discuss it as we meet. Nobody else has it," Evian said, her voice hushed. "If you finish up in time, maybe you can stop by our table and we'll share it with you and maybe even you'll make it on TV."

"Oh, so I'll be on your reality show?" he said. I could see the stars dancing around in his eyes.

"You sure will," Evian said.

I just wanted to say, "Really, dude?" Jay had this look like he would've paid for the chance to be on TV.

"He doesn't need to be on your reality show," I told Evian. "He's a professional, and he's working right now."

"Um, you know, I just may take you up on that offer," Jay said, sliding back from the table. "As a matter of fact, I think we're finished here." Then, this fool actually stood up. "It was good talking to you, Maya. I'll let you know when the story runs."

Evian looked at me, smirked, and then told Jay, "Right this way."

It took everything in my power not to go clean off right there in the middle of that restaurant.

Evian knew she didn't have some exclusive scoop she was working on. Her stupid show had just started airing. But of course, I had to play it cool, so I slowly gathered my things, finished off my coffee, and then made my way out to my car.

"Maya." I turned around to see Sheridan trying to catch up with me. I rolled my eyes and continued to walk toward my car.

"Would you stop?"

I stopped and spun around.

"I'm sorry, shouldn't you be in there filming your *exclusive*?" I snapped.

"Maya, why are you trippin'?"

"Oh, I'm the one that's trippin'?" I said, appalled that she was really going to try and turn this around on me. "My best friend sold me out for her fifteen minutes of fame on a show—that's *not* going to last, by the way. You'll be lucky if you end up on YouTube."

Sheridan looked at me sadly. "Maya, you don't think you sold each and every one of us out?"

"No, and I don't know why you guys keep saying that."

"Because we had a pact," Sheridan said, taking a step closer to me. "We had all agreed that we were going to demand more money and we were working together. You were all on board until they offered you your own show and then you said screw all of us."

I folded my arms and glared at her. "So, like I said, you doing Evian's show is all about getting revenge on me."

"This ain't about you!" Sheridan yelled. She took a deep breath, then calmed herself down.

"Every one of us liked being on *Miami Divas.* Every one of us was sick that the show got cancelled. Do you think I want to be a sidekick, of all things? No, but it's all I got right now. And I think it's foul of you that you don't want anybody else on *your* show but then, you don't want me on anyone else's either."

I was quiet because she actually had a point.

"Again, like you said, this isn't personal," she continued. "I just want my fame just like you."

"Okay, whatever," I said, shrugging. "If you want to attach yourself to a loser, then so be it."

"Right now," Sheridan replied matter-of-factly, "this loser is all I got."

"Whatever, Sheridan." I flung open my car door.

"So, we cool?" she asked, putting her hand on the door.

I really, really wanted to be mad at Sheridan, but I couldn't because she was right. I hadn't given her the opportunity to be on my show and I had bailed on them as soon as I could.

"Fine," I said. "Like I said, you do you."

"But are we cool?" she repeated.

"Yeah, we're cool." I managed a smile. "But just know that when Evian's show flops, I'm not going to let you live it down."

She smiled back. "I wouldn't expect anything else."

Chapter 29

The whole world had lost its mind. That was the only thing that I could conclude as I stared at the spreadsheet laid in front of me. How had Evian's show, which had only aired five times, already be neck and neck with me?

I surveyed the spreadsheet that listed our ratings, which basically told us the number of people who were watching what show. Of course, *Rumor Central* was still number one, but I was dumbfounded that *All American Princess* was anywhere close to me.

"It's the newness of it all," my assistant, Yolanda, said as she set my bottled water down on my desk next to me. I really liked Yolanda because she often knew what I wanted before I even asked for it. And she could read me like a book. Like now, she could tell these rating numbers had me floored.

"This just makes no sense," I said, waving the paper in her direction.

"I told you, it's the newness," she repeated. "That's the only reason Evian has those ratings. People are still caught up in the whole feeling sorry for her. She's still riding that wave. Trust me, it'll drop off."

But what if it didn't? I thought. Of course, I'd never voice that concern. But if they ended up cancelling my show because of hers, I'd never live that down.

"I just can't believe people are watching that mess," I said. "The show is so boring."

"She was trending after last night's show," Yolanda asked. "But it really is because of the kidnapping, not just because her show is all that."

I didn't really know if Yolanda believed that or if she was just trying to make me feel better.

Last night's show hadn't been that bad. But it definitely hadn't been all that. Evian had had a "coming out" party. It was basically to celebrate the "new lease on life" she had after her "near-death experience." Then, the whole exclusive thing with Jay Bee was that she was now working with the National Center for Missing and Exploited Children. She had actually been hired as their spokesperson. I was sick because the whole partying-with-a-cause thing would give her a whole new round of media coverage. I just couldn't believe the luck that kept falling into her lap. It would be different if she were sincere. But I knew that she wasn't. She was just trying to grab fame by any means necessary. I so had wanted to put her on blast and bring up the prostitution ring she used to run with the cheerleaders at Miami High, but since I'd never formally tied her to that story, I decided to leave well enough alone.

"Knock, knock," Evian said, walking into my office before I could say anything. She started waving a piece of paper around. "Did you see the ratings? I'm bringing it," she sang.

"Evian, get out of my office." I pushed my spreadsheet under some papers on my desk so that she couldn't see what I had been looking at.

"Oooh, somebody sounds salty." She giggled, just as her phone rang. "Hold that thought," she said, reaching into her pocket. "That's probably *Ebony* or *US Weekly* wanting to interview me." She pulled out her phone and pushed the TALK button. "Hello, this is Evian," she said, answering in a stupid singsong voice.

Then suddenly, the smile disappeared from her face. She looked at me nervously, then turned and hightailed it out of my office.

"What was that about?" Yolanda asked.

"I don't know," I replied. "But you'd better believe that I'm about to find out." That look on her face—that was a terrified expression, and if something scared Evian enough to stop her gloating, I needed to know what it was. I hadn't made any progress in tying Carson, that guy she'd met at Friday's, and Evian together. I knew there was a common thread; I just hadn't been able to figure it out.

Evian had raced into her office and was now in there with the door closed.

"Go listen," I told Yolanda.

"Huh?" Yolanda's eyes bucked. "What do you want me to do?"

"Just listen," I whispered. "I don't know. Just stick your ear to the door or something."

"Couldn't I get in trouble?" she said. There was no one in the hall at that moment, but it was nothing for several people to be walking up and down this hall at any time.

"Only if you get caught. And if you do, make up a story. You said you want to be a fiction writer."

Yolanda seemed hesitant, but then said, "Okay." I watched as she walked down the hall to Evian's office door and held up her hand like she was about to knock, then she leaned in to listen.

I stepped back in my office because I didn't want anyone to see me watching Yolanda. I busied myself, continuing to study the ratings sheet because something had to be wrong. Maybe the ratings people had mixed up some numbers. After a few minutes, Yolanda stepped back in my office.

"Okay, I almost got busted, but I did hear her. She's going off," Yolanda said.

"Going off on who?" I asked.

"I have no idea, but they were arguing and she said something about not giving him any more money and to leave her alone."

I fell back in my seat. My antenna was definitely up now.

Suddenly, we saw Evian speed-walk past my office, still looking frazzled. She had her purse on her shoulder like she was about to leave.

"Nah. Something is definitely up," I said, trying to figure out what to do. Finally, I said, "Let me borrow your car."

"Huh?" Yolanda said as I held out my hands.

"Here." I reached over on my desk, snatched up the keys to my BMW, and handed them to her. "Roll in style for a little while. Just be careful. What kind of car do you have?" I asked as I hurriedly grabbed my purse.

"A Pinto."

"What's a Pinto?"

"It's a brown car, a Ford, kinda old, a little raggedy. It's parked at the front of the building."

I wanted to ask her why in the world she'd be caught dead in something like that, but I was in a hurry.

"Cool, I'll be super careful in your Pinto," I said sarcastically, as I raced out the door behind Evian.

Chapter 30

I guess that I had learned a thing or two hanging around WSVV because I was in full investigative mode. I couldn't believe I was rolling in this dump of a car (I made a mental note to ask for a raise for Yolanda because NO ONE should be forced to drive some crap like this). But it was serving its purpose. No way would Evian notice me in this hoopty.

I was keeping a short distance from Evian. This girl was up to no good and I was determined to find out what was going on.

Evian pulled into the parking lot of Dunkin Donuts and eased her Range Rover into a handicapped parking spot. (I thought about calling the cops to report her, but I didn't want to get sidetracked.)

She seemed on a mission, and I know she wasn't in that much of a hurry to get a dang donut.

I parked and waited for her to go inside; then I pulled out my cell and punched in Alvin's number.

"Hey," I said once he answered.

"Hey," Alvin replied.

"What are you doing?"

"Working. What are you doing?"

"I'm following Evian," I whispered as I ducked down in the car.

"Following her where?"

I kept my voice low. "Right now, she's getting a donut, but I can tell she's up to something. Maybe she's meeting that guy from Friday's."

"Why are you whispering?" he asked.

"Because it's a top-secret mission," I said. "I don't want her to know I'm following her."

"But aren't you following her in the car? Alone?"

"Yeah."

"So, again, why are you whispering?"

I thought about what he was saying, then burst out laughing. "Oh, my bad." This girl was making me crazy.

"Girl, you are too much," Alvin said. "But what are you trying to do? Why are you following her again?"

"I'm just trying to find out what she's up to. She got a call, then rushed off. It's something fishy going on."

"What, your Spidey senses are tingling or something?" he asked.

"You can make jokes all you want, but she's up to something."

I watched as Evian walked back outside. "Un-unh, I told you that she was up to something," I said, back to whispering. "She doesn't even have any donuts." I eased down in my seat some more as Evian glanced around the parking lot. She was really looking all irritated, like she was somebody. I know people said that I was full of myself, but I had reason to be. Evian had her nose all up in the air for no reason.

Evian almost looked like a crack fiend, waiting on someone to deliver her fix, the way she was fidgeting. I didn't know what was going on, but she was clearly agitated. I watched and waited. Just like I'd done at T.G.I Friday's. She finally stopped fidgeting when a gray Honda Civic pulled into the parking lot.

Her eyes stayed fixed on the car as the driver pulled into the parking lot. She didn't move until finally, she walked over to the car. Whoever was inside, didn't get out. She approached the window. It looked like they were exchanging words; then Evian stomped off.

I couldn't be sure, but it almost seemed as if she was crying.

She got back in her car and I contemplated whether I should follow her or the driver of the Civic. I decided that she had to tape a show, so I knew where she was going. I needed to know who was in that car, so I followed the Civic as it pulled out of the parking lot. I could see it was a guy, but I couldn't get close enough to see who it was. But thankfully, before he got on the freeway, he turned into a gas station. I eased into the parking lot behind him. I hadn't been able to see who he was as he went in so I parked next to his car to wait for him to come out.

When the door to the store opened, he walked out on the telephone.

"Yeah, I met with her. She's trippin' for real. She . . ." He almost dropped the phone when he saw me. I guess he was as stunned as I was.

"Well, if it isn't Mr. Carson Wells," I said.

"M-Maya," he stuttered. "Long time, no see."

As soon as he spoke, I knew his voice. The same voice that had answered when I'd called. The same voice that had said his name was Miguel.

I didn't know whether to go off, or turn and leave, but my need for answers made me say, "I don't know what kind of game you're running, but I have the strangest feeling it's no good." I glared at him, waiting for an answer.

He looked around the parking lot. "Not here." He pointed across the street. "Follow me over there to the Starbucks."

I raised an eyebrow. I know he didn't expect me to follow him anywhere.

"It's a bunch of people in Starbucks—I'm not going to do anything to you. I know you want some answers. Follow me over there and you'll get them."

I guess my need to connect the dots was greater than any fear, because I just nodded as I got back in my car to follow him to Starbucks.

Chapter 31

I couldn't believe that I was actually face-to-face with Carson Wells. Or Miguel, or whatever the heck his name was.

"Hey, beautiful," he said, like were meeting for a date or something.

"Really?" was all I could say as I stared at him from across the corner table where we were sitting.

He shrugged and slid in the seat across from me. The Starbucks where we were meeting was filled with the hustle and bustle of people trying to get their java fix. But all I cared about was this snake in front of me.

"So, is this your game? You're a con artist?" I said.

"No, not that at all, what I am though," he said with a sly smile, "is an opportunist and an opportunity just fell into my lap, so I took it."

That piqued my interest, although I didn't know how much to believe of what he told me.

"I have a lot of questions," I said.

"I may or may not have answers," he said with a grin.

I studied him, trying to see through the lies. "How about I start with what's your name? Your real name?"

He smiled. "Miguel. Miguel Cantone."

I shook my head. "Why lie, Miguel Cantone?"

He shrugged nonchalantly. "It's what I do when I pick up chicks."

"So, are you even a student?"

"Nah," he said, chuckling. "I dropped out of school in the tenth grade."

"How old are you?"

"Twenty-two."

I felt disgusted to my stomach. I'd almost made out with a twenty-two-year-old high school dropout?

"Wow, so you just travel to Cancun and try to pick up teenagers?" I asked.

"No, Cancun is actually home." He shrugged indifferently. "I'm a native. But I'm back and forth here all the time, which is why I don't sound like I'm from Mexico. I just happened to be home at the time you guys visited."

"And you *happened* to meet me and said, 'Oh, here's a sucker I can run game on'?"

"Not at all," he replied.

"So, why didn't you tell me the truth?"

"Hey, it's like you said—I didn't know you like that. Look, I'm sorry to stress you out behind all of this. I was just trying to get with a beautiful girl and then I saw a quick way to make some money," he said. He put his hand on the table and covered mine. "But you have to admit, we have some kind of chemistry."

I jerked my hand away. "I don't have to admit anything except that you turn my stomach." I looked him dead in the eye.

I decided that I didn't really care what his real name was anyway or whether he was a student. I was just grateful I hadn't done anything with him in Cancun. So, I asked the question I really wanted to know. "What's going on with you and Evian?"

He paused, looked like he was thinking, then said, "I'm not ready to answer that one just yet." He had the nerve to smile at me.

"That's the question I really want answered," I said firmly.

He nodded, then said, "What do I get for telling you anything?"

"You get me not blasting you all over TV," I snapped. "You get me not going to the police."

"You're some kind of piece of work, Maya Morgan." He reached up to touch my hair. I jerked my head out of his reach.

"Just answer the question, whatever your name is."

"I told you my name is Miguel." He leaned back, thought for a minute, then said, "Cool, ask me whatever."

I leaned forward. "Let me ask you, *Miguel,* how are you and the guy I saw Evian with the other day connected?"

"Pedro? Oh, that's my cousin," he said matter-of-factly.

Pedro, I thought, *where have I heard that name before?*

"Pedro," I said slowly. "Wait a minute. Is that the guy that was holding Evian hostage? I mean, where we rescued her from? The guy at that place where we found Evian?" I remembered why he looked familiar now. That little boy that was the lookout, the one that thought we wanted to buy drugs when we went to rescue Evian had said Pedro was inside.

He laughed. "I guess you're not at the top of your game for no reason." He winked. "I've done my homework on you."

That creeped me out, and once again I said a silent prayer that he had nothing to blackmail me over because I had no doubt he'd try to use it.

"But yeah," he continued, "Evian was at Pedro's place in Cancun."

"You say that like she was there willingly."

He hesitated again, and I could tell he was thinking about just how much he was going to tell me. Finally, he said, "Screw it. She wanna play me, I told her she'd regret it."

My heart started beating fast. Was I really about to get the truth?

"They paid Pedro to help them fake a kidnapping. He's the one that called you guys about the ransom. The one whose house she stayed at. My cousin."

"So, you were in on this from the jump?" I asked. "Was the guy you dared her to go with part of your scheme?"

"Nah," he replied. "I didn't know him. My boy Princeton told your girls I was a local and they hit me up for help."

"Was this before or after you were trying to get with me?" I asked pointedly.

"It was after you kicked me to the curb, the night on the beach." He raised an eyebrow like this was my fault. *Really, dude?*

"During Spring Break Fling, my boy who works at a local hotel hooks me up with a room, so I can, ah, hang out . . ."

"And pick up chicks?" I said with disgust.

He obviously wasn't fazed by my dig. "Yep, and pick up chicks." He shrugged again. "Anyway, Princeton must've told Shay where I was staying because she was at my hotel waiting on me when I got back from . . . ah, being with you."

I wanted to say, "You mean, got back from dang near attacking me," but I simply said, "Why should I believe you?"

He nodded like he understood that. "You don't have to believe anything I say." Then, he removed his phone from his pocket, set it on the table between us, then tapped the screen. He swiped until he got to the VOICE MEMOS button. He opened it, pressed play, then pushed it toward me.

"Just believe what you hear," he said as the recording started playing.

"Sorry, I needed to take that call. So tell me again what do you want me to do?" That was Miguel's voice.

"Look, your boy told me that you're from here. That he's visiting you."

"Is that Shay?" I asked.

"Just be quiet and listen," he said, smiling.

"Okay, and?" Miguel asked as the tape continued playing.

"And we need some help," Shay continued. *"Princeton said you could help us."*

"Who is we?"

"My girl Evian."

"So she came back?" he asked.

"She never left," Shay replied. *"But we need it to seem like she did."*

"So what kind of help you need from me?" He sounded tired and I recalled how buzzed he'd been that night.

"We need someone we can trust. Someone that can help Evian lay low for a day or two," Shay said.

"Lay low how?"

Shay sighed like she was frustrated. *"We are runnin' a little game of our own and we need someone that is willing to help us make it look like Evian has been kidnapped."*

"Whoa, we just get chicks and do small hustles." Miguel sounded like he'd perked up now. *"That's some major stuff you're talking there."*

"You're not really kidnapping anyone," she said. *"We just need you to help us make it look like a kidnapping. We need a local place for her to be found."*

"Aww, man. I don't know about that. Why are you guys doing this?"

"You don't worry about why we're doing it. Just help us out and we'll make sure it's worth your while."

There was a brief silence. I leaned in closer so I could hear better.

"Worth my while how?" Miguel finally said. *"What do I get out of it?"*

"How is five grand?" Shay replied.

"Not as good as ten."

"Ten thousand dollars? Really?"

"Look, you're asking me to put a lot on the line, carry out this deception, find someone to help you out, then I have to split whatever I get with him." Miguel sounded fully sober now.

Silence again. *"Okay, cool,"* Shay finally said. *"Seven grand."*
"Ten."
"Fine," she huffed

"Where's your girl now?" he asked.

"She's in the room, but we have to sneak her out."

"All right," he said, *"I'll call my cousin. He'll help us hook everything up. You can take her over there tonight. But if the cops get involved in any of this, I'm telling everything."*

"I will make sure the cops don't get involved," Shay said. *"You just do your part."*

"Cool, get your girl and meet me out front in twenty minutes," he said.

Miguel pressed stop, then picked the phone back up. "You don't have to believe me, but believe that."

I sat there, absolutely stunned. "So what made you record your conversation?"

"I told you." He dropped the phone back in his pocket. "I'm an opportunist, always looking for an opportunity, and I know you always have to have insurance. And the fact that she was at my hotel waiting, I knew something wasn't right. So the minute she started talking, I acted like I had a phone call, so I could press record and get the whole conversation recorded."

"So, why are you here now?"

"Because they're trying not to pay. They gave us three grand in Cancun and they were supposed to send the rest when they got back to Miami. Not only did these chicks stop taking our calls, but I find out your girl is using the whole thing to blow up." He leaned back. "So, that meant the price had to be renegotiated. Me and Pedro hightailed it here. Evian gave him the rest of the ten grand, but she didn't want to agree to our new terms. I warned her. So, the way I see it, if she doesn't want to pay for this"—he patted his pocket where he'd dropped his phone—"maybe you will."

"Oh, so that's what this is about? Getting more money. That's why you agreed to talk to me?"

"Yep." He flashed a smile. "Is this recording worth ten grand to you?"

He just didn't know. I'd pay twenty for that recording, but I just said, "Let me see what I can do. I might know some people who would be interested in buying it from you."

"Cool, I'm only in town a few more days." His grin got wider. "It's the college spring break next week and I need to get back to Cancun."

I wanted to throw up in my mouth. He was truly a slimy snake. I shook off that thought and focused back on the issue at hand. Miguel had just handed me the perfect opportunity to bring Evian down. Now, I just needed to figure out how to utilize it.

"So what do we have to do now?" he asked.

"We don't have to do anything but go our separate ways. I got your number."

"How?" he asked, shocked.

"Because I'm Maya Morgan." I stood up. "I'll be in touch when I'm ready for you."

I turned and headed toward the door.

"Hope you don't make me wait too long—for my money and a second chance with you," he called out after me.

I almost turned around and laughed in his face, but I thought it was just best to ignore him as I kept it moving.

Chapter 32

Evian was cold busted and I was about to let her know that I was hip to her game. I'd tossed and turned all night, trying to come up with the perfect way to bust her. But ultimately, I decided it would give me great pleasure just to march into Tamara's office and give them the recording. It's a good thing we were out of school today, because I don't know that I could've made it through the whole day without calling her out.

I'd called Miguel this morning and told him that I would have his ten Gs tomorrow. Of course, he'd been thrilled.

I leaned against the doorway of Evian's dressing room and just stood there until she noticed me.

"May I help you?" she finally asked. She spun around in her chair, crossed her legs, and glared at me like she was Oprah and I was barging into her mansion.

"Oh, just wondering if you want to return the favor," I casually said.

"What are you talking about?" she snapped.

"You know, I was just wondering if you wanted to help me like I helped you."

"Maya, what are you talking about? I really don't have

time for your games. In case you haven't noticed, I have the hottest show on TV right now and I'm pretty busy."

I ignored her delusional comment and sashayed into her office. She'd set up shop like she'd been here for years. There were pictures of her and every celebrity under the sun. I almost asked if they were Photoshopped because yeah, right, she was all snuggled up with Usher. That was probably an Usher impersonator.

"I saved you, remember?" I said, running a finger along her dressing table. "You were a damsel in distress. A nobody. Until I plucked you from those kidnappers' arms and made you relevant."

She released a laugh. "Really? *You* made *me* relevant." She spun back around to face the mirror and started applying her lip gloss. "Girl, you should be a comedian. I think they're hiring down at the Just Jokes Comedy Club."

I eased down onto the leather sofa in the corner of her office. "So, have you talked to Carson lately?"

She stopped and stared at me from the mirror before slowly turning around.

"Who is Carson?" she asked.

So she really was going to try and play this all the way left?

"Carson. From Cancun." I snapped my fingers. "Oh, I'm sorry. His name is really Miguel."

"What?"

I stood up, tired of playing around with her. "Don't what me, Evian. Was this some kind of game you guys were running all along? Were you playing me from the beginning?"

She picked her lip liner up and began slowly lining her lips. "I have no idea what you're talking about."

I spun her chair back around. "Cut the crap, Evian. I know everything. Now you either admit what you did or we can go have this conversation with Tamara and Dexter."

She glared at me but didn't say anything. Finally, she set

her lip liner down and crossed her arms. "You would love that, wouldn't you? You'd love to do whatever it takes to bring someone else down. What's the matter, Maya, you afraid of a little competition?"

"Ha! Afraid of you? Get real. I just don't appreciate getting played. And that's exactly what you, Shay, Carson-slash-Miguel, Pedro, and everyone else in on your jacked-up plan tried to do."

"It was your idea to do the dumb truth-or-dare game."

I walked over to the wall, where she'd hung up the framed *People* magazine article. "So, what happened, you went for a stroll and decided, 'hey, let me pretend to be kidnapped'?" I asked.

She gave me a blank look before saying, "And so what if I did?"

"Really, Evian? I don't understand how you could have everybody freaking out about you, and you were running a big ol' scam."

"Look"—she crossed her legs like she was about to read me—"I didn't plan it. I went off with that guy and he put something in my drink."

I looked at her skeptically. "How do you know he put something in your drink?"

"I saw him." She shot me an evil glare like it was my fault. "Now, had I not seen what he was trying to do, this story could've turned out very differently. But I did see it, and just as I was about to come back down to the beach, I figured you guys had no problem placing me in danger. I might as well *be* in danger."

"So, there never was a kidnapping?" I asked point-blank.

She smiled and shrugged. "There could've been."

"So, I guess you called Shay and had her in on all of this." Her smugness was straight pissing me off.

"You can assume whatever you want. I'm done talking to you." She spun back around and finished putting on her makeup.

"Wow. Just wow," I said. "The lengths some people will go to for a little bit of fame."

"Wow, for real." Evian laughed, before picking a handheld mirror up off her dressing table and turning it toward me.

"What's that for?"

"You need to be looking at yourself and telling yourself those words because you wrote the book on what someone is willing to do for a little bit of fame."

"Whatever," I said. "Let me just go see how Tamara feels about this whole deception."

I spun around, but before I could reach the door, she said, "Because we both know that snitching is the only way you can beat me."

I stopped and turned back to face her. "Excuse me? So what are you trying to say?"

"I'm not *trying* to say anything. I'm saying it." She stood up and took a step toward me. "You think you're all that, but I'm this far"—she stepped so close to me that our noses were almost touching—"from stealing your star."

I took a step back. "Are you freaking kidding me? You couldn't take my star if I wrapped it in a big box with a bow and handed it to you."

She shrugged, then turned to go back to her seat. "Hmph. Whatever. Run along." She waved me off like she was telling me to shoo. "Go snitch so I can let everyone know that you were so threatened by me, so worried that I would take your top spot, that you had to snitch in order to beat me."

Oh, she was straight challenging me now. I didn't care about the whole no-snitch ghetto mentality, but she'd gotten me riled up with that comment. If that's the way she wanted to play it, I had something for her. I knew that she was just trying to keep me from telling. But I definitely didn't need her or anyone else thinking that I felt threatened in any shape, form, or fashion.

Now that I thought about it, I wasn't going to tell

Tamara. Yet. As a matter of fact, I was going to enjoy demolishing her.

"You know what?" I said. "I won't tell because I want to see the look on your face when they kick you back on the curb where you were before I made you relevant."

She spun around again, stood, and stretched out her hands like she was challenging me. "Bring it."

"Brought it," I replied. I was so going to bring it. And when all was said and done, Miss All American Princess was going to wish that she'd never crossed me.

Chapter 33

"So, what do you think?" my friend Zenobia said. "Should I use this one or this one on my invitations?"

I snapped myself out of my daze and turned my attention back to her stack of senior portraits. They actually were very beautiful, but they reminded me that not only had I not even taken mine, I hadn't even ordered my graduation invitations. Yes, we still had eight weeks before graduation, but all of my friends had already taken care of all of their senior responsibilities. I wasn't doing a very good job of balancing everything. And as I glanced across the cafeteria at Shay, Evian, and Sheridan sitting in a corner table, I knew exactly why I was slipping.

"You know what, Maya?" Zenobia said, pulling her pictures back. "Maybe I need to attach some juicy gossip to the pictures, then you'll want to give your input."

"I'm sorry, Zenobia. My mind just isn't here."

"It never is," she said, stuffing the photos back in her bag and walking away.

It's not that I was that close to Zenobia, but she and I were cool. So, any other time, I would've been happy to give her my opinion, but today, my head just wasn't in it.

I glanced back over at Sheridan, Shay, and Evian, and it dawned on me that I used to be cool with a lot of people, but for some reason, I was losing them all.

Sheridan lost her smile as I approached their table. I needed to tell her she didn't need to fake it with me. Obviously, she enjoyed kicking it with Evian and Shay. She didn't need to pretend otherwise for my sake.

"Hey, Maya, you can sit here," Sheridan said, moving her purse from the seat next to her.

"Naw, I'm good. I'm going to go sit over there." I motioned two tables over.

"Yeah, let her go sit over there," Shay snarled.

I glared at her, then said, "You know what? On second thought, I will sit here." I dropped my tray on the table next to Sheridan and sat across from Evian and Shay.

"So, Shay, what's up?" I wondered if Evian had told her that I was on to them. Judging from the defensive look on her face, like she didn't know what my next move would be, Evian had definitely told her.

"Everything's everything," Shay said. "On top of the world with my girl."

We all glared at each other, but nobody said a word.

"Did your girl tell you that you're about to be toppled?" I asked.

Neither of them said a word as they just shot evil daggers at me.

"Okay, does somebody want to tell me what's going on?" Sheridan said, looking back and forth between the three of us. "I know you all have beef, but this seems like it's on a whole different level."

"Yeah," I said, cocking my head, "somebody want to tell her what's going on? What's *really* going on? Since you guys are all BFFs now."

Before anyone could reply, our English teacher, Mrs. McAfee, approached the table.

"Miss Matthews," she told Sheridan, "did you forget about the Honor Society meeting today at lunch? It looks bad that everyone but the president is there."

"Oh, snap," Sheridan said, quickly standing up. "I forgot." She started gathering her things. "I'm on my way."

Mrs. McAfee shook her head as she grabbed her Coke and walked off.

"Guys, I have to go, but somebody needs to let me know what's going on later," she said.

"Oh, you'll find out soon enough," I said before she scurried off.

Silence once again filled our table. Finally, Evian spoke. "So, I see you decided not to tell on me."

In my opinion, she needed a little more gratitude in her tone.

"No, I haven't told. Yet. I wanted to prove that your show sucks before I prove what a liar you are," I replied.

Shay rolled her eyes. "I told you, Evian, don't sweat her. She can get up there and say what she wants about us. It's not like anyone will believe her because everyone knows she's jealous of you."

I couldn't do anything but shake my head. "You got it so twisted. Maya Morgan doesn't have to be jealous of anyone," I told her. "And you forget, it isn't just my word."

Shay turned up her lips. "Oh, yeah, a scam artist with a criminal record. I'm sure *everybody* will believe him."

Wait? Criminal record? So I'd almost got with a twenty-two-year-old high school dropout who ran game and picked up chicks, and who had a criminal record? I shivered at the thought.

"As far as I'm concerned, you're a jealous diva that's mad because my girl is about to knock her off her throne," Shay continued. "So now you're making up stories, claiming the kidnapping didn't happen."

"Oh, is that what I'm doing?" I asked. I came so close to letting her know about the recording, but I decided that I didn't need to be showing my whole hand. "We'll just have to see who they believe, won't we?" I said.

"Look, Maya," Evian said, in a totally different tone like she was trying to change the direction of this conversation. "I'm sorry we dragged you in this, but you know how hard I worked to get in the entertainment industry. You know all the freakin' auditions I've been on, and how hard I worked. And nothing. This situation in Cancun—"

"The *fake* situation in Cancun," I said, cutting her off.

"Whatever," she replied. "What happened in Cancun gave me what no amount of training, auditions, or anything else ever could. It gave me instant notoriety. I don't understand why you can't respect the game."

I looked at her like she was crazy. "Because I can't appreciate being played."

Shay continued to glare at me. "Don't apologize to her, Evian. I told you, she would've done the same thing to you. Shoot, she probably would've done a whole lot worse."

I turned my attention to Shay, really looking at her, trying to understand why she hated me so much. Sitting across from her at this very moment, I knew one thing: any progress I had made with Shay over the past few months was out the window. She had the nerve to be staring at me like she was so innocent and I was the one out of order.

"So, you don't see anything wrong with the way you played me, the way you had me running around Cancun looking for Evian, stressing? I mean, good grief, you had me trying to come up with ransom money," I told her.

"Which you made it clear that you weren't going to do."

"Because five hundred thousand dollars is a lot of money," I snapped. "But I was trying to come up with what I could."

My mind raced back to all the times Shay had seemed so hysterical and scared for Evian, how she'd made us miss the senior breakfast, and how it had messed up my spring break.

"How could you just act like that?" I asked.

Shay shrugged. "I guess it's just natural talent." She put her hand to her chest as she got all dramatic. "Maya, I know where Evian is. The GPS tracked her," she said, mimicking her actions in Cancun. "Maya, we have to save her."

She giggled like she was really funny.

"I guess you got a good laugh out of that," I said. "You found it funny that I was willing to put my life on the line to save her," I added, jabbing a finger in Evian's direction.

"Whatever. Don't hate because I'm so convincing." Shay put a finger to her head like she was thinking. "Maybe I need to call Tyler Perry and have him put me in his next movie since I'm such a good actress." She laughed and it made my blood boil.

I stood up. "I'm glad you think this is funny." I looked back and forth between the two of them, then walked over to the trash can at the end of the table and dumped my uneaten salad inside and set my tray down. I walked back in front of them, picked up my purse, and said, "But we're going to see who has the last laugh," before strutting out of the cafeteria.

Chapter 34

I had given my all to *Rumor Central* this past week, and at this
very moment, it felt like none of that mattered. I had spent all
week digging for an exclusive, some blockbuster story for my
show that would get people talking. Kennedi had been
adamant that I should get the tape from Miguel and play it on
my show. And although I hadn't ruled that out, I wasn't ready
to do it just yet. I wanted there to be no doubt that I was
number one, and I didn't need anyone thinking that I only
retained that spot because I had gotten rid of Evian. And I
knew that's exactly how she would play it. So, although I'd
met Miguel and given him the ten grand for the recording,
I'd put it up to use as a last resort.

I'd never expected that that last resort might be needed
right now.

"Maya, this is a serious problem," Tamara said, snapping
me back to the reason I'd been summoned to her office as
soon as I got to work today. "Everybody has been noticing
how you're not seeming like yourself lately."

"I don't know why anyone would say that," I replied.

"It's just that you don't seem on top of your game. You

seem distracted," Tamara said. "And while I know you guys tried to clean up that disaster at the *Hype* magazine Teen Choice Awards, that was so not a good look. The old Maya would've never got herself caught up in some drama like that."

What was I supposed to say? Tell them that I'd become so obsessed with finding out what was going on with Evian that my own show was suffering? That she got under my skin so bad that I'd let her knock me off my A game? Naw, never that. But I knew that I needed to say something.

"I guess it's the balancing of it all. Trying to get ready for graduation and everything," I said, trying to sound sad so she would be sympathetic.

She was sympathetic all right. But not in my favor. "If this is too much for you to handle, let us know," she said.

I raised an eyebrow. "What is that supposed to mean?"

"Oh, Maya, don't read anything extra into it," Tamara said.

I decided to stop beating around the bush and come right out and ask them. "So, are you guys planning to cancel my show?"

"No," Tamara said. "There are no plans to cancel *Rumor Central*, but . . ."

It was the way she said "but" that had my stomach turning flips.

"But what?"

"But if you continue on this track, the higher-ups will not be pleased. I told you everything was about ratings. You didn't come back from Cancun with much."

"That was your and Dexter's idea in the first place," I protested. "Besides, I had Evian's story, since you all think that's such a big deal."

"Yes, you did. But none of the other celebrity stuff that we thought we'd get panned out. Word is that TMZ is running a story that they got the same time you were in Cancun. Apparently, rapper Jay Blackmon was there with Darian Mathis? I mean, he's only one of the biggest rappers and he's in Cancun with another woman, and you missed that?" She shook her head like she couldn't believe it. "TMZ is supposedly running a big exclusive on it, and we're trying to figure out how that one just slipped through your fingertips."

I groaned inside. I wouldn't dare tell them that no, I hadn't missed it. I'd just gotten sidetracked trying to help Evian. Yet another reason for me to hate her. I'm about to lose my job over messing around with her, and it was all a scam. I felt my blood boiling all over again.

"We are just wondering if you have what it takes to keep *Rumor Central* afloat," Tamara said candidly.

"Excuse me?" Now, I had an attitude. "I made *Rumor Central* the hit that it is."

"We don't dispute that. But we're not into creating one-hit wonders."

"I can't tell," I said. "With *All-American Princess*, seems like you guys are banking on a one-hit wonder." I wasn't trying to be disrespectful, but this was ridiculous.

"The bottom line is her ratings are going up and yours are going down."

I couldn't believe this. I wanted so bad to tell her what I'd found out about Evian, but she definitely would think I was just trying to say something. Besides, Kennedi was right about one thing: If Tamara knew Evian was a fake, she'd try to save face for the station and would make sure this went away quietly. If I did decide to bust Evian, I needed it to be grand, for the whole world to see.

"Well, don't worry, I have something major in the works," I told her. "And I assure you, once it hits, it's gonna be big."

"I hope so," Tamara said. "You know I like you and it would break my heart if we had to cancel *Rumor Central*, but

I have to put you on notice. Either come up with some major stories or we're in some major trouble."

I nodded. Oh, I was about to give her something major. She wasn't going to like it, but she was definitely about to be served ratings on a silver platter.

Chapter 35

"Wow. I go away for a conference for a week and all this happens?"

Alvin leaned back in disbelief as I filled him in on the events of the past week. He was surprised at what Tamara had said, but he wasn't worried. That was one of the things I loved about Alvin: he believed in me no matter what.

"So, you mean Evian really faked all of this? For fame?"

"Yep, that's what her show needs to be called, *Faking it for Fame*." I was sitting on Alvin's living room sofa. When I'd arrived this afternoon, his mother had been here and I'd gotten a chance to talk to her for a little bit, something I rarely got to do because she was sickly and stayed secluded in her bedroom most of the times I came over.

"Dang," Alvin said. "This is all just so wild."

"Tell me about it," I said.

"So why did this Miguel guy just decide to come clean to you?"

That was the part of the story Alvin definitely wasn't feeling. He said it was bad enough that I had given him any money, but he definitely didn't think I should have any more conversations with him.

"It was all about money," I said. "But I've been giving this some thought, and it's actually the real reason I came over here to talk to you today. I think I'm going to fly Miguel back to Miami to help me out."

"What?" Alvin said, looking at me like I was crazy. "Help you out with what?"

"I told you Tamara wanted a blockbuster story. I'm about to give it to her."

He shook his head like he was adamantly opposed to that idea. "You know he's all about money."

I shrugged. "Then I'll pay him. I couldn't care less about him getting his money, but even if I just play the tape, I will still end up looking like a hater. But if I can figure out a way to get him to do it . . ."

"I don't know, Maya" Alvin said. "I think you should just leave this alone. You have the tape. That's enough to prove she's a fake. This guy may be dangerous."

I don't know why, but I wasn't really scared of Miguel. I saw him as fairly harmless, and nothing more than a con artist. "I can't let Evian get away with this."

"Seriously, Maya, I think you should just let this beef with Evian go. Just let Tamara know the kidnapping was a fake, she'll cancel the show and you'll have won."

"Are you crazy?" I told him. "The way this girl has barged into my life, the way she ruined my spring break, had me running around like crazy, looking for her and she wasn't even missing. Oh no, I'm going to enjoy paying her back."

He sighed like he knew it would do no good to try and talk me out of anything. "So what exactly are you going to do?"

"That part I haven't figured out yet," I said.

"What do your girls have to say?"

"Of course, Kennedi is down for whatever I want to do, and I'm not telling Sheridan anything." There was a part of me that was still mad at Sheridan's betrayal, but there was also a part of me that understood. I knew I would get over it. I always did when it came to Sheridan, but she would find out what a faker Evian was right along with everybody else.

"You think Sheridan will tell Evian if you have something planned?" Alvin asked.

"I don't know," I replied. "I mean, I don't think so." I didn't think Sheridan would tell Evian anything, but with Sheridan, you just never knew and I wasn't going to take that chance.

I fell back against the chair. This whole day had been exhausting.

"So what are you doing tonight?" I asked. It was a Friday night, and after that meeting with Tamara, I felt like maybe I needed to get out and relax, enjoy myself.

"I'm going to the Jay Z concert tonight. Remember, I got those front-row tickets?"

"Oh, yeah. I forgot." I stood up. "Let me go home and change."

An uneasy look crossed his face. "Ummm . . . well, I had, I mean, when I didn't hear back from you I kinda sorta just asked Marisol to go with me."

I stood frozen, staring at him. "I texted you back," I finally said.

"Umm, no you didn't," he replied.

"Well, I meant to."

"Look, Maya, it's cool."

"Are you kidding me? You know I love Jay Z. And you're taking her?" My day just kept getting worse.

"I am," he said. He had a look on his face like he couldn't believe my nerve.

It looked like he was waiting for me to get jealous again. I had something to show him. I composed myself and said, "Well, you guys have fun," as I headed toward the door.

"Maya," Alvin said as he followed me. "Why do you keep getting mad at me behind Marisol?"

"Naw, I'm not mad," I said, as I kept walking. "I'm cool. I have a bunch of work to do anyway."

I kept moving, making my way through his living room. I had just reached the front door when he grabbed my arm.

"Maya."

I stopped but didn't turn around. And before I knew what was happening, Alvin turned me around, leaned in, and kissed me, on the lips, hard.

I don't know if I was more shocked or impressed.

"My heart belongs to you," he said. "And when you're ready for me, I will let Marisol and everyone else go."

"Everyone else?" I found myself saying as a sinking feeling built in my stomach. "I mean, umm, I will call you later."

I was speechless as I made my way out to my car. I couldn't get Alvin's kiss off my mind. Was I . . . ? Could I . . . ?

"Nah," I told myself as I climbed into my car. Alvin was like a brother. I didn't care if that kiss was one of the best I had ever had. He wasn't my type.

My phone rang and shook me out my trance. I pressed the answer button as I backed out of the driveway.

"Maya?"

"Yeah, this is Maya," I said. I'd been so frazzled that I hadn't even checked the caller ID to see who it was.

"Hey, it's Lorna from Publicity," she said

"Oh, hey, Lorna. What's up?"

"Sorry to call you so late on a Friday, but I just wanted to let you know that Kevin Smithers from *The Insider* will be taping live from Miami Monday afternoon and they're hoping to do an interview. Please tell me you can do it."

"If I wasn't available, I'd cancel whatever I had," I told her. "Of course, I'll be there."

"That's awesome. But um, it's, ah, it's actually for you—" She hesitated. "It's for you and Evian."

I wanted to scream. Now Evian was elbowing her way into my interviews?

"They're doing this whole competition thing," Lorna continued. "The two hottest shows on the market. We tried to tell them it's not a competition, but they want to interview you both at the same time."

I was just was about to protest when it hit me. Opportunity had just fallen in my lap.

"Oh, it's cool," I said, a wide smile crossing my face. "I don't mind doing the interview with Evian."

"You don't?" Lorna sounded shocked, like she'd been expecting a fight.

"Nope, it should be fun," I said.

"Well, great then." Lorna rattled off the details. After I hung up, I took a deep breath and dialed Miguel's number. I finally had a plan for exactly how I would bring that *All American Princess* Evian Javid down. I just hoped I could get Miguel back to Miami in time. But somehow, I believed that with the right amount of money, that was something I didn't have to worry about.

Chapter 36

It felt good to be on the other side of the microphone. As much as I liked interviewing, I loved being interviewed just as much. I plastered on a smile as I waited for *The Insider's* host, Kevin, to introduce me.

"Good evening and welcome to *The Insider*. I'm your host, Kevin Smithers, and can I just tell you, I am so excited about today's show."

Kevin just didn't know, I was excited, too. When I'd offered Miguel an airline ticket and another five grand, he'd been all too happy to hop a plane and come right over. He'd arrived early this morning. And then, I'd found out yes, this was going to be taped, but it was still airing tomorrow, which meant *The Insider* interview would air two days before my *Rumor Central* blockbuster story. Things couldn't turn out better if I'd planned it myself.

"We have a rarity on today," Kevin said. "Any of you that have been following entertainment news know there's a battle brewing between two of the hottest teen starlets in the country."

The camera panned out to me, standing to the right of Kevin, then to Evian, who was on Kevin's left.

"Maya Morgan, host of *Rumor Central*, and Evian Javid, from the reality show *All American Princess*, are with me today. Now, in this day and age, we know there's more than enough room for entertainment news and reality TV, but we wanted to make sure you were aware of a little background on both of these women."

He took a few minutes and played a clip of my show and then of Evian's wack show. The red light came back on signaling that Kevin was back on the air.

"Now, Maya Morgan has been around for a little bit longer than Evian."

"A lot," I said, not losing my smile.

Kevin chuckled but kept talking. "But Evian has burst onto the scene."

Evian tossed her hair over her shoulder and grinned as well.

"But the question is, which one of these ladies will come out on top in the ratings game?" Kevin said. "And we've garnered an exclusive with the two of them to talk about why they think they have the hottest shows and how they plan to capture the title of Teen Queen Supreme. We'll do that right after the break."

Both of us kept our smiles plastered on as the show went to commercial. We tried everything to make sure we kept it cordial even though I wanted to punch her in the eye. But no need to do that, I told myself. She would get hers in due time.

"So we're straight?" Kevin said, looking back and forth between the two of us like he was worried something might jump off. "We don't want a repeat of the *Hype* Teen Choice Awards."

"Oh, we're good," Evian replied.

"Yeah, I just had a manicure. I'm not interested in getting my fingernails dirty by touching her," I replied.

"All right, all right. Well, let the claws come out." Kevin laughed. "I'm sure both of you know claws make for good TV."

We laughed, but there wouldn't be any claws, at least not on my end. *She* may be ready to attack though before the end of our interview.

"I want to ask both of you, what's the secret to your success?" Kevin asked once the camera came back on.

We spent the next five minutes talking about what made our shows unique and why viewers should tune in. Kevin also asked about our own relationships and how it felt going from members of *Miami Divas* to arch enemies.

"Well, in order to have an enemy you have to feel threatened and Evian's a sweetie pie. Not threatening at all." I could tell she didn't like that comment because she glared at me even though she kept her smile.

"And Maya understands that it's only so much selling out of your celebrity friends you can do before people stop confiding in you," Evian said. "I try to keep it classy."

"Ouch," Kevin said. Before I could respond, though, he turned to me. "We are almost out of time. But Maya, I understand that you have a little surprise you'd like to present to Evian."

"I do. A little something I stumbled upon." I had to struggle to contain my enthusiasm. "I know her reality show is about her new lease on life since escaping her abduction. She hopes to serve as an inspiration for all those who have overcame, so I want to take a moment to introduce you to a young man who's overcome quite a bit."

Evian looked at me and then back at Kevin. I know she was trying to figure out who I was talking about; that's why it was my pleasure to give the signal for Miguel to come walking forward. (He'd made it very clear that although he told me his real name, he wanted me to refer to him as Carson in the interview.) I'd had to tell *The Insider* producers what I had planned, but once they got the story, they were all too happy to let me do this.

"I met this young man in Cancun. I thought that he was a little cutie," I said as he walked onto the set.

"Uh, I *am* a cutie," Miguel replied.

"That you are," I said, giving him his props. I wanted to add that he was a thirsty drunk, too, but I let that slide.

Miguel stood next to me as I continued. "Well, I brought him on so that he could tell you the little scam he and his cousin were a part of in Cancun."

I turned to face Evian and saw the look of horror on her face. I could tell she was contemplating whether she should run or stay and try to talk her way out of it.

"Welcome to the show, Miguel. Please, do tell."

Miguel looked at Evian and smirked. "Told you you shouldn't have crossed me," he told her before turning to Kevin. "So, Kevin, it's like this. My cousin and I are always looking for a come-up from the tourists to Cancun. So, when one of them came to us wanting to help make it look like she'd been kidnapped, we were all for it."

Kevin's eyes perked up. Evian was frozen in place.

"A fake kidnapping," Kevin said, finally looking back at Evian.

"This is crazy," she said, finally speaking up. "I thought this interview was supposed to be about me and Maya and our shows."

"Oh, it is," I interrupted. "Because you see, I was the one that discovered her when she was kidnapped," I told Kevin. "My whole spring break was ruined because we were running around the island, panicking, trying to find her. Then, her friend Shay Turner miraculously got a lead on where she was. I was gung ho to go in there and save her. I thought I was putting my life in danger, but I was willing to do that"— I smiled at Evian—"for a friend. So we went in to save her. And we did. Or at least we thought we did."

"So, wait a minute," Kevin said. "You mean to tell me that Evian wasn't really kidnapped?"

Evian started removing her mic, which was clipped to her shirt. "This is ridiculous," she said, standing up. "I refuse to stay here and listen to these lies." She threw the mic on the floor and took off running out of the studio.

Kevin glanced at her, but turned his attention back to me.

"So, is that what you're saying?" he repeated.

"That's exactly what we're saying," I answered.

"So there really was no kidnapping ring in Cancun?" Kevin asked.

"Not that I know of," Miguel replied.

"Why are you coming forward?" Kevin asked.

"Let's just say, the whole plan requires commitment on both ends. And the end that was supposed to take care of me and my cousin, didn't. So, I'm singing like Tyrese. Besides, I like Maya. I was kinda a creep to her when we first met."

I smiled, surprised at his admission.

"Wow, this is stunning to say the least. So all the hoopla, all the media coverage for Evian's kidnapping, was based on a hoax?"

"Seems that way," I replied. There were so many things I wanted to say about Evian and her sheisty need for attention, but this was one of those times when I felt like silence was truly golden. The less I said, the better. I'd exposed her for the fraud that she was. I'd let karma do the rest.

Kevin turned back to the camera. "Well, you heard the exclusive here first, only on *The Insider*." He put his finger to his ear like he was listening to someone tell him something. "And just for the record," he continued, "my producers just told me that they've done some fact-checking and Miguel's story seems right on the money. Of course, we're going to stay all over this story, as I'm sure everyone else will." He turned to me. "Including you. Right?" he said, jokingly.

"You know it," I said. "In fact, for those that doubt what I'm saying, tune in to *Rumor Central* tomorrow. I'll have something they won't want to miss."

Kevin's mouth dropped open. "Are you sure we can't get that now?"

"Sorry, Kevin. If they want the real scoop, they'll have to tune in to *Rumor Central* from here on out."

I smiled at the camera as Kevin wrapped up the show. The first part of my plan was complete. Tomorrow, I'd top it all off with the tape. I couldn't help but smile. Evian should've never told me to bring it, because she should have known that I definitely would.

Chapter 37

People were going to learn that when it came to going up against Maya Morgan, you really shouldn't.

There was a reason I was on top of my game. Because I was straight, no faker, and that's exactly the way Evian had hoped to ride all the way to the top. Faking it.

I couldn't believe that I actually felt a little bad about that *Insider* interview. I'd heard that Evian had burst out of the studio in tears. She hadn't been at school today and was probably in hiding. Everyone at school was talking about the *Insider* interview. And it was a trending topic on social media. Yet, blasting Evian out so publicly hadn't given me the joy that I'd thought it would.

I shook off any sad thoughts I had and turned my attention back to the camera. I was right where I should be—hosting my show. I was number one in the game, and Evian was where she should be—at home sulking, or wherever she was. I really didn't care.

"So, are you ready?" Tamara said, approaching me. I had expected her to be furious with me. And she had been, for a minute. But then, when I'd told her about the tape, her thirst for ratings had overridden any anger.

"Aren't I always ready?" I replied.

Tamara gave a half smile. "That you are." She paused, like she was waiting on me to say something. "Go ahead," she finally said.

"Go ahead and what?" I casually asked.

"Say I told you so," Tamara said. "I know you want to say it. I know it's just eating you up." She grinned at me.

All American Princess was no more. As soon as I'd gotten to the station today, I'd heard that the show had been pulled, effective immediately. Evian's star had not only fallen, it had straight nose-dived. It hadn't even been forty-eight hours since that interview, and the network had pulled the plug on her show. It probably didn't help that every media outlet under the sun was running a story about the fake kidnapping.

I smiled back. "I don't have to say it." Then I winked at her. " 'Cause you already know it."

"Hey, in this ratings game, it's all about winning. That's all I was trying to do with Evian." She shrugged.

"But you already have a winner with me," I said, holding my hands out and doing a quick pose.

"That I do. Sorry about how everything went down."

"It's cool," I said. "I understand that it wasn't personal, it was business." I could say that now since I'd come out on top, but Tamara didn't have too many more times to be underestimating me. I was on top for a reason.

"And stand by." Manny gave me the cue as Tamara ducked out of the way.

"What's up, everybody? It's your girl, Maya Morgan. I'm here with the scoop, and today we're digging up dirt on my former friend, the *All American Princess* herself." I paused. Something just didn't feel right. I had revamped this intro and I had planned to tear all into Evian, but for some reason I just couldn't. I saw Manny looking at me confused and I quickly composed myself.

"Well, I'm sure many of you have seen the story in the

media or heard how Evian's kidnapping was revealed to be a hoax." I paused again. This was where I planned to play the tape, let them hear where it all went down. I had worked it out with the audio department and they knew exactly when to roll the recording. But for some reason, I couldn't give them the cue. "Ah, we know the kidnapping was fake," I repeated, before pausing again. Finally, I said, "But I've since learned that it wasn't a complete lie."

Tamara stopped and I could see her looking at me strangely from behind the camera. I don't know what came over me but I continued.

"Although Evian wasn't kidnapped and held against her will as she led the world to believe, she came dangerously close. Evian saw someone trying to slip the date rape drug into her drink. Luckily, she caught him and the danger of the date rape drug is something we definitely need to explore in a future episode. So, although there was no kidnapping, her story could've been tragic. Now, if Evian is guilty of anything, it was capitalizing on an opportunity. In this world of Internet sensations, she used that moment to catapult her fame. I can't even be mad at her," I found myself saying, "because in this day of YouTube, Vine, and Instagram, this is the way to garner instant fame. No one cared about the years of hard work that she'd put into trying to break into the entertainment industry. No one cares that she's been modeling and trying to get gigs since she was three years old. Forget the acting classes, the networking. These days, all it takes is a video camera to make an instant star. And Evian, like so many others, got caught up in the hype. I know her, we go way back. She's cool people so you guys cut her some slack. I know I did."

I tossed the rest of the papers detailing my plans to go in depth and expose Evian's story.

"But in the meantime I've got some *real* dirt to tell you about." In the midst of everything I had going on, I'd gotten a call yesterday from Savannah Vanderpool, a former Miss Teen Miami who had gotten caught up in a drug ring. She was out, clean and sober, and ready to talk to none other than *Rumor Central*. So, I would just tease that story. "So don't touch the remote," I continued. "You'll get the scoop right after this."

The music came up as they went to commercial. Tamara came racing over. This time, Dexter was with her.

"What are you doing?" Tamara asked.

"I don't know," I said. "I just don't want to call the girl out like this. I just couldn't go through with it."

Dexter's mouth fell open. "What? I heard the tape. You're not going to play that?"

"Nah. It's irrelevant."

Tamara stared at me in shock, too. "Oh my God, Maya. So are you getting a conscience?"

"I guess," I replied. "I just know that she feels bad enough as it is. Her show is gone. She can't show her face. No need to beat her down anymore."

"So, does that mean you won't mind having her as a cor-respondent on your show?" Dexter asked.

"Uh, no, I didn't say all that. She needs to stay as far away from the TV as possible, but maybe from time to time we can let the former *Miami Divas* make an appearance on my show. As long as everybody doesn't get it twisted and forget who the *real* star is."

"Not that you would let any of us forget it," Tamara said.

"Believe that." I winked as I went to finish my show.

Chapter 38

I felt better than I had felt in a long time. I was back on top with my show (not that I was ever *not* on top, but there was no longer anyone there nipping at my heels).

Yesterday's episode of *Rumor Central* had been one of my highest-rated shows ever. Yeah, I had a lot of complaints that I hadn't dished the dirt, but the fact remained that they'd tuned in.

So between that, the fact that I'd aced my world history test (don't even ask me how I'd managed to do that), and now this, I was feeling pretty good.

This was simply dinner.

But there was nothing simple about the fact that my whole family was sitting down to dinner together. It felt like we were a real family. My dad, who seemed to have been gone for the past two months (he was opening a luxury hotel and spa in New York), was home for his birthday. We were having a birthday dinner. My mom claimed that she had done the cooking, but she wasn't fooling anyone. I'd seen her favorite catering truck leaving when I got home today. But I was going to let her have her moment. I think my dad was hip to her as well because he kept raving about how he didn't know that she knew how to cook shrimp linguini.

"Never underestimate your wife," my mother said as she, my dad, Travis, and I sat around our long rectangular dining room table. The food was spread out in the center and looked fit for a king.

"I know," my dad said. "I've learned over the years that my wife is capable of doing whatever she sets her mind to." He winked at me.

"All I know is this is some good eating. So may I have seconds please, Aunt Liza?" Travis said as he held his plate out.

"Of course you may," she said, handing him the pasta. I don't know what it was about Travis, but he brought out another side of my mom—a kinder, gentler side—and I liked it. She seemed more relaxed. More fun.

"So, Maya, did you fill your father in on your first-class handling of the Evian situation?" my mother said.

"Yeah, sweetie," my dad said. "Your mom told me about all of that. I can't believe that girl would fake a kidnapping."

"No, what's even harder to believe," Travis interrupted, "is that Maya had the chance to blow her out the water and didn't take it."

My father laughed. "You know I'm all for being ruthless in business."

"Well, honey, you have to be," my mother said, patting his hand. "You don't amass a slew of hotels by not being ruthless. And while I'm glad our daughter has that trait, it makes me proud that she also knows when to rein it in."

My dad nodded. "I agree. Success is the best revenge. You succeed on your own and don't worry about anyone else. That's the best way to blow someone out of the water."

"Yeah, I know," I said. "I learned from the best."

We laughed and talked some more as my dad told us about his New York hotel. We were really having a good time.

That was why none of us paid any attention when the security system buzzed, letting us know that someone was at the gate.

"Mom, did you give Sui the day off?" I asked after the third buzz.

"Oh, I did. Can you go see who that is?"

"Oh, so now I'm the maid," I said, even though I backed up from the table.

I looked into our security camera system and was shocked at who was out front. I punched the code to open the gate and met her at the front door.

"Evian?" I said as she came up the walkway to my front door.

"Hey, Maya," she replied.

I leaned against the doorway. I know she didn't think she was coming into my house. "Um, what's up? I mean, to what do I owe this pleasure?" I hadn't seen Evian all week. She hadn't been at school. I'm sure she was too ashamed to show her face. Shay, on the other hand, had bounced in like nothing was wrong. However, although she would never say it, her attitude had been a little less stank and she hadn't been as rude. I think she was just grateful that I hadn't put her on blast as well.

Evian twisted her purse strap as she talked. I could tell that she was extremely nervous. "Look, I know it's taken me a minute, but I just wanted to come and say I'm sorry. For everything. I was only thinking about myself and I hate that I ruined your spring break. I mean, I'll pay for you to go on a vacation somewhere else."

I looked at her crazy. "Yeah, I can pay for my own vacation. That's not the point. Everything you and Shay did was foul."

"I know that now. And I am really sorry . . ."

I stood and let her ramble her apology.

". . . and you don't ever have to forgive me, but I just want you to know that I am grateful. I can only imagine what things would've been like if you had played the tape."

"You weren't on the tape. Shay was," I told her.

"Yeah, but it could've really messed her up and then I would've felt bad that I ruined stuff for her, too." She let out a long sigh. "Miguel told me that he taped everything. He said you had the tape. You just didn't play it on the air. So as bad as things were, I know they could've been a whole lot worse. So thank you."

There were a lot of things I could've said. A lot of things I thought about saying, but all I said was, "You're welcome. And we're good." I didn't ask why she was talking to Miguel. I didn't really care. As far as I was concerned, my business with him was done. He'd headed back to Cancun and I didn't care if I ever saw him again.

"Okay, that's all I wanted. I guess I'll see you at school Monday. I'm coming back." She shrugged. "Can't hide forever." Evian stood for a minute, and then when she saw I really didn't have anything else to say, she waved, then walked back to her car.

I couldn't help but smile. Yes, I could be a little ruthless, but when all was said and done, Maya Morgan had a good heart.

I turned around to see my mom, Travis, and my dad, standing in the living room staring at me.

"I am so proud of you, baby girl," my dad said.

"Me, too," my mom added.

"If I hadn't seen it, I wouldn't believe it," Travis added as we all laughed. "My cousin is going soft."

"Don't get it twisted. I go hard—but only when I need to." I sashayed past my family and back toward the dining room. "But come on, you guys. Let's go finish off this white-chocolate cheesecake mom bought . . . I mean, made." We all settled back at the table. "Let's toast," I said, raising my glass of iced tea. Everyone else did the same. "To my family," I said. "Tonight, I'm not Maya Morgan, the superstar. Tonight, I'm just Maya Morgan, daughter, cousin, and all-American princess."

Everyone laughed as we sipped our drinks. I loved this feeling—the feeling of being on top of the world!

TRUTH OR DARE

ReShonda Tate Billingsley

ABOUT THIS GUIDE

The following questions are intended to
enhance your group's reading of
TRUTH OR DARE.

DISCUSSION QUESTIONS

1. Was Maya wrong not to tell her friends from jump that she would be filming in Cancun? What should she have done differently?

2. Cancun was all about having a good time, but do you think the group went too far when they began playing truth or dare?

3. Why do you think Bryce is always there when Maya needs him? Should she stop being so bitter toward him?

4. Should Maya have insisted that they call the police from the beginning? Why do you think she didn't?

5. What are some of the clues Maya should've seen that told her something wasn't right about the whole kidnapping caper?

6. Before giving Evian her own show, Tamara approached Maya about having her appear on *Rumor Central*. Do you think Maya should've just let Evian be a correspondent?

7. Maya was extremely upset about Sheridan appearing on Evian's show. Do you think she was justified in her anger? Should Sheridan have appeared on the show?

8. Maya became consumed with Evian to the point that her own show was suffering. Why do you think she was so wrapped up in Evian?

9. Maya always runs to Alvin to help her out of binds. Alvin never complains. Do you think Maya is denying her true feelings for Alvin? Should he wait for her, or move on?

10. Ultimately, Maya didn't play the tape and put Evian on complete blast. Why do you think she had a change of heart? Do you think she should've gone ahead and played the tape?

Rumor Central continues with
Boy Trouble

Coming in October 2014
Wherever books and eBooks are sold

Chapter 1

Membership had its privileges. Membership in the "It Clique," that is.

"Maya! Are you and J. Love back together?" the photographer shouted in my direction, just as the flash went off.

It didn't take long before security was all over him, dragging him and his camera out.

I kept my signature smile, but I didn't miss how everyone was staring my way. Oh, yeah, I loved my life as the go-to chick in the entertainment industry. And I didn't even need to be in L.A. to claim that title. I was kicking butt and taking names from right here in Miami.

I, the fantabulous Maya Morgan, had made a household name of myself as host of *Rumor Central* and though many had tried to knock me off my throne, no one had succeeded. That's why I was once again sitting in the VIP with the hottest rapper in the country by my side, and paparazzi sneaking in, trying to get my picture.

I glanced over at J. Love and he winked. I knew he was on cloud nine, because he'd been trying and trying to get me to give him a second chance. Long story on why we broke up in the first place, and I wasn't trying to give him another chance.

But J. Love didn't get where he is by taking no for an answer. He kept after me and I finally broke down and agreed to go to this MTV party that we'd both been invited to. One of my BFFs, Kennedi, was here, too, even though I hadn't seen her butt in the last thirty minutes.

I knew the paparazzi would eat it up if they saw me and J. Love back together. And I was right on the money, too, since the man they had just escorted out was trying desperately to keep taking pictures as they tossed him out.

"Hey, babe, you need anything?" J. Love asked as he stood. We both were used to the paparazzi, so it really wasn't that big of a deal.

"No, I'm good," I replied.

"You sure you don't want something to drink?" he asked me again. He'd been trying to pump liquor in me since I'd walked in the door. "This is some good stuff," he added as he held up his cup. I turned up my nose. I didn't need to drink to be cool. I'd said it before and I'll say it again. I don't need anything to take me off my A game.

I glanced to my left and saw a girl passed out in a booth in the corner—her legs were gaped wide open and someone was taking a picture of her. She would be on YouTube before she woke up. No, that wouldn't be me. I worked too hard to build the Maya Morgan brand and I wasn't going to blow it over a glass of Patrón.

"No, J. Me and my water are just fine," I said.

"That's why your skin is so beautiful," he said, smiling at me. "All that water you drink."

I smiled. I wanted to say, *Tell me something I don't know*, but I'd been trying to curb my confidence since *Teen People* had recently done an article calling me "arrogant." I couldn't help it—I was all that. And I knew it. But Tamara, my boss at the TV station, suggested I bring the confidence down a notch.

"Well, well, well, if it isn't Miss Maya 'Snitch' Morgan."

I turned around to the voice coming from behind me. I rolled my eyes at the sight of the one person in the industry I simply could not stand: actress Paula Olympia.

I couldn't stand her because she couldn't stand me and she made sure to tell anyone who would listen how she really felt about me. Paula had been on a hit TV show eight years ago, but her star had definitely fallen. So, I didn't sweat that one-hit wonder and her funky attitude because as the comedian Katt Williams said, "If you don't have haters, then you ain't doing your job."

"What's up, Paula? Nice dress," I said, looking her up and down. "Isn't that the new collection at Target?"

She put her hands on her hips and wiggled her neck. "Whatever, Maya." She held her hand up as if she was blowing me off, before turning to J. "What's up, J.?" she said, smiling flirtatiously.

"It's all good," he said. Either he was blind and dumb, or he was just trying to ignore her while he was acting like he couldn't tell she was flirting with him.

"How you been?" Paula smiled again as she fingered his chest. My eyebrow rose.

"I'm cool." J. Love stepped away from her and over to me. "Um, hey, babe, I'm going to go and get something to drink," he said, making a hasty exit. Guess he wasn't so dumb after all.

"Anything else I can help you with?" I finally told Paula. She was messing up my mood.

"No, I'm just saying hello," she said with an attitude. "Waiting on my boo."

"Okay, but why don't you go wait on your *boo* somewhere else?" I said, turning back to look out on the dance floor.

"You know you're always asking for the scoop. Maybe you'll want this one," she said.

As if I'd want anything Paula Olympia had to offer.

"Paula, if it involves you, I'm good," I told her.

She ignored me and kept talking. "I just thought you'd like to know that Demond Cash and I are an item."

That made me do a double take. Demond Cash—the A-list actor? What he wanted with her D-list behind was beyond me, but I wasn't going to let her see that I was fazed.

"Okay, good for you," I finally replied. "When you become somebody that is worthy of being on my show, I'll look into that. Until then, later." I stood and pushed her aside. If she wouldn't leave, I would. I made my way around the club to see if I could spot Kennedi. I also needed to see if I could roll up on some dirt. I was always in gossip girl mode, and since this party had everybody who was anybody, I was bound to find some dirt up in here.

I saw one of my old friends and went to talk to her for a few minutes, and then decided that I needed to get back to the VIP because this being down here with the common folk wasn't cutting it. I made my way back up the stairs and had just rounded the corner when I saw J. Love and Paula deep in conversation.

"What's going on?" I said, approaching them. J. Love jumped back, but Paula let out a smile.

"Just sitting here, catching up," she replied.

I looked at him and crossed my arms. If he told me he used to date Paula Olympia, I'd be too done.

"So, you're going to give me a call sometime?" Paula asked him.

"Uh, nah, I'm good." J. looked nervous as all get-out.

I couldn't help it—I stepped in her face. "Really, Paula? Like seriously, you want to go there?" I told her.

"My, does the little girl feel threatened by a real woman?"

I didn't know how old Paula was—the tabloids said she was twenty-two, but I'd bet a hundred dollars she was at least thirty-two.

"I would never be threatened by your desperate behind."

I usually didn't do any arguing over a guy. Period. But Paula had rubbed me the wrong way.

"Rawr," she said, making a clawing motion in my direction. "Sounds like the cat is jealous."

"Jealous of you? Get real."

This party was definitely becoming whack. Now that I knew they'd let Paula Olympia in the VIP, it was changing my perspective on everything.

We stared at each other as Demond approached. "Yo, what's up?" he said. "Is something wrong?" He looked back and forth between the two of us. "Hey, Maya Morgan," he said, recognizing me. "What's going on?" He stuck his hand out to shake my hand. I didn't take my eyes off of Paula.

Demond's gaze shifted back and forth between us as we glared at each other.

"Okay, what's up?" he asked.

"Your date is what's up," I said, not taking my eyes off of her. This one-hit wonder was about to learn I was not the one to mess with.

Demond put his arm around her. "What is my girl over here doing?"

"You need to get 'your girl' before she gets slapped." I was never one for violence, but I wasn't about to be played either, especially when I was sure someone around us was rolling on their camera phone.

"Oh, who's going to slap me?" Paula asked.

"Disrespect me again and see. You know J. Love is here with me and you got one more time to roll up on him . . ." I wasn't even into J. Love like that, but I could just see the headline: PAULA PUNKS MAYA. No, ma'am.

"Yo, hold up, what?" Demond said, dropping his arm from around her neck. "What do you mean roll up on your man?"

"Nothing baby," Paula said, pulling his arm. She suddenly no longer looked confident. She actually looked, I don't know, scared.

"No, what's she talking about?" he asked, jerking away.

"I'm talking about your girl right here flirting with my date, trying to get his number so they can go out, while you're just across the room." I turned my lips up in her direction. Yes, I just cold busted her.

"What?" Paula acted shocked. "Babe, she's just running her mouth. Don't listen to her."

Demond's happy demeanor had disappeared and he looked burning mad. He didn't say a word as he grabbed her arm and pulled her out of the VIP and toward the back.

J. Love just stood there like he didn't know what to say or do. Kennedi, who I hadn't even seen approach, leaned over and said, "You think you should've done that?"

I side-eyed her. "Girl, please. In the words of Kevin Hart, she gon' learn today," I said, before picking up my bottled water and returning to my seat.

Chapter 2

It was time to call it a night. Paula had ruined the mood and I hadn't even been able to enjoy myself the past fifteen minutes. J. Love was trying his best to get me to go to some after party with him. But I was a little salty with him because while he hadn't encouraged Paula, he'd done nothing to shut her down. That wasn't a good move for him. He was already on my bad side because of the way we'd broken up. He'd treated me like crap when somebody had told him that I'd leaked something to the press. Turned out it was a hacker/stalker, but the fact that he hadn't even given me the benefit of the doubt had severely damaged our relationship. Every time I tried to give him another chance, he did something like this to make me mad. But I couldn't deny the fact that J. Love was all that and then some. Not to mention the fact that his record was the hottest joint in the country right now. Still, I'd blessed him with my presence enough.

"You ready to go?" I asked Kennedi.

"Yeah," she said. She'd been in a foul mood herself most of the evening. I think it had something to do with her new boyfriend, Kendrick. Even though she kept denying it, she really wanted to go out with him tonight since she'd just gotten back in town. (Kennedi, my BFF since like forever, had just moved back to Miami from Orlando.) But Kendrick had had to go *out* of town, so Kennedi had been stuck hanging out with me. When she'd told me that, I had straight given her the side-eye. Nobody had to be *stuck* doing anything with me. It was a privilege to be with Maya Morgan. But since she was my BFF and I knew she was mad at Kendrick, I'd let her make it.

"Yeah, let's go," Kennedi said.

I said good-bye to J. and promised to call him later. He wanted me to wait so he could walk me out, but his manager wanted him to meet some bigwig at MTV and I didn't feel like waiting.

"I still can't believe they had a party with no valet parking," I said as I thought about the two-block trek we had to pick up my car. "Where they do that at?" I moaned. I probably needed the exercise. I had missed my Pilates class this week so I sucked it up.

Kennedi and I joked about some of the people at the party as we were walking. We had just rounded the corner when Kennedi stopped and grabbed my arm. "Isn't that your girl?" she said, pointing.

I looked to the right and saw Paula and Demond deep in conversation and he did *not* look happy. In fact, he leaned in front of her and jabbed his finger in her face.

"Whoa," Kennedi said, pulling me back so they couldn't see us.

"Oh, snap!" I replied as I fumbled to get my iPhone out of my clutch. Paula and Demond were going at it. Oh, I was definitely about to record this. Now that iPhones were in high definition we could easily use this video on my show. I stepped to the side and zoomed in as much as the camera would go as the two of them argued.

"Dang, I wish I could hear what they were saying," Kennedi whispered.

"Shh!" I motioned toward her. I didn't need any extra noise in my video.

"You got me messed up!" Demond screamed. That definitely was loud enough for us to hear. It was what happened next that almost made me drop my camera phone. He hauled off and hit Paula so hard he sent her hurtling to the ground. He then reached down, picked her up by her hair, and slammed her up against the wall.

While I desperately wanted to keep filming, that was one thing I couldn't stand: a guy putting his hands on a girl. So, I knew that I needed to step in.

"Hey, what's going on?" I asked, stepping around the corner.

Demond glared at Paula, but did release her. She scrambled to pull herself together.

"Is everything all right?" I said, walking up to them.

"What's up, Maya? I was just having words with my girl," Demond said.

"Are you all right?" I asked, looking at Paula.

Paula cut her eyes at me. "Why don't you mind your own business?" she snapped. "Oh, I forgot, your janky behind doesn't know how."

"Wow," I replied, my eyes fluttering in shock. "I'm over here trying to keep you from getting your behind beat and you want to snap on me?"

"Like I said, don't worry about what's going on over here," she said, glaring at me like I was the one who just Floyd Mayweathered her behind.

I couldn't believe this chick. I actually had to stop and do a double take. Then I threw my hands up.

"I hope you have a good night," I said, before turning and stomping off.

Kennedi turned and took off after me.

"She's lucky I don't fight," I huffed. "Because I'd knock her in her other jaw."

"Calm down," Kennedi said. "They're just having beef. That's all."

I shook my head as we neared my car. "You better believe you're going to see this on *Rumor Central* first thing Monday morning."

"Maybe you shouldn't do that," Kennedi said.

I stopped and stared at her. Since when was *she* the one trying to worry about someone's feelings, especially someone like Paula Olympia?

"Really, K?" I said. "Did you not just see the way she acted toward me? And this was *after* she tried to push up on my man earlier."

"You said yourself that you don't even like J. Love like that."

"She totally disrespected me."

"So? It's not like you're in some gang or something. I'm just saying leave it alone."

I looked at my friend and raised an eyebrow. Yeah, Kendrick had her all messed up because there's no way the Kennedi I knew would ever have let something like that go.

"All I'm saying," Kennedi continued, "is that you should . . ." She stopped speaking midsentence as her gaze went across the parking lot.

I turned to see what she was staring at, but there was no one there but a guy and girl cuddled up against a black Escalade.

Kennedi squinted in their direction, then mumbled, "Oh, I don't think so," before stomping off toward the couple.

"Kennedi, what's going on?" I asked, scurrying to catch up with her.

She didn't say anything as she stomped across the parking lot like a girl on a mission. I had no idea what had my BFF in a rage, but I took off after her, determined to find out.